crossing into brooklyn

crossing into brooklyn

Mary Ann McGuigan

MeritPress

Avon, Massachusetts

Published by
Merit Press
an imprint of F+W Media, Inc.
10151 Carver Road, Suite 200
Blue Ash, OH 45242. U.S.A.
www.meritpressbooks.com

ISBN 10: 1-4405-8463-X
ISBN 13: 978-1-4405-8463-3
eISBN 10: 1-4405-8464-8
eISBN 13: 978-1-4405-8464-0

Printed in the United States of America.

10   9   8   7   6   5   4   3   2   1

Library of Congress Cataloging-in-Publication Data

McGuigan, Mary Ann.
   Crossing Into Brooklyn / Mary Ann McGuigan.
      pages cm
   ISBN 978-1-4405-8463-3 (hc) -- ISBN 1-4405-8463-X (hc) -- ISBN 978-1-4405-
8464-0 (ebook) -- ISBN 1-4405-8464-8 (ebook)
   [1. Family life--New York (State)--New York--Fiction. 2. Secrets--Fiction. 3. New York
(N.Y.)--Fiction.] I. Title.
   PZ7.M47856Cr 2015
   [Fic]--dc23
                                    2014047032

This is a work of fiction. Names, characters, corporations, institutions, organizations,
events, or locales in this novel are either the product of the author's imagination or, if
real, used fictitiously. The resemblance of any character to actual persons (living or dead)
is entirely coincidental.

Many of the designations used by manufacturers and sellers to distinguish their products
are claimed as trademarks. Where those designations appear in this book and F+W Media,
Inc. was aware of a trademark claim, the designations have been printed with initial capi-
tal letters.

Cover design by Frank Rivera.
Cover images © kmichal, Aleshyn_Andrei/Shutterstock.com.

This book is available at quantity discounts for bulk purchases.
For information, please call 1-800-289-0963.

To Don, for being right there with me when I finished painting this, and for encouraging me to give this silly habit more time and attention. Thank you.

To Matthew, Douglas, and Jess, the only fan club I'll ever need.

Also by Mary Ann McGuigan

Morning in a Different Place
Where You Belong
Cloud Dancer

one

The closet smelled of my mother's perfume, of her absence, the part that lingered when she left for Baltimore or Atlanta or Chicago. It was everywhere, inescapable. It clung to the designer suits on their curved hangers, shoulders slouching, like whipping boys. You could see it in the shape of her shoes, lined up like yes men, ready to swear to her lies.

I couldn't find her precious project notes. She'd spend weeks on them when she was putting a proposal together. She kept them in little spiral-bound notebooks, had one with her all the time. I checked every drawer, every shelf, every bag. Nothing. Could she really have taken it with her, even to Grandpa's funeral?

I stepped out of the closet, into the huge bedroom. The house was quiet, but my parents would be back any minute. The funeral luncheon was almost over when I got my cousin to drive me home. My mother didn't see me leave. She was talking to my father, which had to be a first. The wake for Grandpa went on for two days and I never saw them speak the whole time. The three of us mostly stood in our dreary little reception line as people wandered in and greeted us with weak handshakes and loose hugs. They kept their coats open, ready for a speedy exit, and I wanted to follow them out the door, get out of my damn heels, get away from the whole mess.

Even before Grandpa got sick, my parents were doing their talking behind closed doors. The night before the funeral, I heard them in their room. What a sight I made, kneeling outside, my ear to the door, desperate. I could hear only bits and pieces. My grandfather needed a kidney. My mother was not a match. I knew all that. But my father kept telling her it wasn't her fault he didn't make it. It just didn't add up.

That's how I wound up searching her bedroom. I wanted papers from the hospital, from the doctors, anything that could tell me what the hell she was up to. But most of all I wanted to find her damn project notebook and shove it down the garbage disposal. After the Mass, as we got into the car, she told me she was going ahead with her trip to Chicago. What would it have taken to disrupt my mother's business trips? Clearly Grandpa's dying wasn't enough. My soccer playoffs, two days away, didn't even rate a mention. In the limousine, she reached for my hand as we passed through the cemetery gate. I stared out the window, pretended not to notice.

I opened the dresser drawers again, checked the jewelry box. Nothing. I was running out of time. I headed back to the closet, wanting to do something spiteful, defame the immaculate order of her little shrine to executive apparel. That's when I noticed the briefcase tucked behind her velvet chair, its polished leather sides reflecting the light. It had two compartments that opened like an accordion, both crammed. I walked my fingers through some folders, pressing open one or two. No notebook.

A side pocket was zipped closed. I pulled the zipper along its track, smooth and silent. The compartment was deep, and I couldn't see anything. I slipped my hand into the tight space, felt something tubular, wrapped in plastic. A tampon. I slid my fingers toward the other side, and found a paper folded small and tight. I pulled it out and opened it up. A letter. But it had been torn up, the pieces taped back together. Some of them were missing, leaving holes where the words used to be. The handwriting was large, a little shaky. The first few words were gone:

". . . when Michael Mulvaney passed away." Then something about a house, but most of that was blurred into the folds. Only two sentences were still whole: "If you could find it in your heart to come and talk, it would mean the world to him and to all of us here. Brooklyn is not so far after all." Then one last fragment: " . . . he asked for you to the end, M&M." There was a date in the corner, September 19, and it was signed by someone named Clover.

Nothing in the note made sense. I didn't know anyone named Clover. Who was Michael Mulvaney? And why did they want to talk to my mother? I reached into the side compartment again. This time I found a photo, a picture of my grandfather and me, taken when I was eleven. He looked healthy and strong. The pain of missing him came back in a rush, as if out of hiding, into my chest, into my throat.

What my mother did or where she went didn't hurt as much before. But Grandpa was gone now, and my parents were even more distant, hardly speaking—to me or to each other. He'd been dead less than a week, and already I had trouble picturing him. I needed photos, and there weren't many around. Our whole museum of a house had only two framed photographs: one of my parents on their wedding day and another of me—the official annual portrait of Morgan Lindstrum, in perfect hair, perfect dress—taken the year before, when I was fifteen. Photographers were paid to take both, and the work was done in a studio, the results touched up. My parents didn't have much interest in seeing things the way they really were.

I was sick of all the pretending, all the secrets. That morning, after I got dressed for the funeral, I went downstairs to talk to them. They were standing in the kitchen and I asked them point-blank what it was all about, why my mother wasn't a match to donate a kidney. "Blood types aren't necessarily a match, not even between parent and child," my mother said, but she wouldn't look at me.

"So that's all it was? You didn't have the right blood type?" I said.

"Yes."

"Then why did you have to tell her it wasn't her fault?" I said to my father. He started to answer, but my mother cut in. She would do the talking, as usual.

"You must have misunderstood," she said. "No one said that."

My father busied himself with his phone. She was lying, and we both knew it.

I wanted my grandfather. He was never too busy for me. He was even upset that he couldn't go to my playoff game. Like he didn't have enough to worry about, with all the tubes and wires they had him hooked up to by then. When Dad was teaching at the University of Chicago, Mom started traveling more, but Grandpa looked after me. He liked to take me to the library. He listened to my complaints about school, made sure I brought gloves when it was cold. He was never pressed for time, never on his way to somewhere else. In the end, after we moved to Princeton, I was the one who had no time, no need to sit down with him, to walk to the coffee shop to get the paper the way we used to on Sundays. I had new friends by then, places to go.

I looked at Grandpa in the photo, smiling at the camera from behind my shoulder, his arms around my waist. I recognized the watch on his wrist. I closed my eyes and remembered how the long gray hairs curled around the gold. When he lost all the weight, he didn't want to wear it anymore and gave it to me. The night he died, I took it out of my jewelry box and fell asleep with it beneath my ear, pretending I was resting again against his chest, against his heart beating.

two

I got the D train at Herald Square, just a block or two out of Penn Station. It was such a strange feeling to know I was sitting beneath all those huge buildings in lower Manhattan. A voice called out stations—West 4th Street, Broadway-Lafayette Street—but the words were erased by the rattle and shrill of the wheels, jamming and forcing their way over tracks that took us farther into the darkness. Just a turn or two after we left Grand Street, the train moved beneath the gray waters of the East River—almost quietly, as if stunned by the weight of the water—and suddenly I was crossing into Brooklyn.

The train smelled of burnt dust, and the unpredictable screeches and twists kept my whole body tense in the hard plastic seat. I gripped the warm metal pole near the door and tried not to stare at the people sitting stiff and sullen across the way. I'd never seen so many shades of skin in one place before or heard so many accents. I was a little embarrassed, although there was no good reason to be. I was the only female in the car, except for two women wearing uniforms and long sweaters, and I didn't see any other teenagers. But it was more than that. I felt frivolous. The men's hands were calloused, their work boots worn down. My Burberry scarf matched my bag in a way that now seemed gauche. The train from Princeton to Penn Station that morning hadn't been all that crowded, but it had almost all white people on it, people who didn't look so worried.

At 25th Street, I got off the train, just as the man from the cemetery had instructed. The street was busy, and I felt anonymous. The cemetery wasn't far, only a block away.

I turned in at the open gate, walked slowly, looked for the turns the man described. I tried hard to dismiss the thought that I'd forget my way back and be stranded there. I headed for the top of the hill. The day was sunless now and getting colder, the ground hard. Sharp, dry weeds pulled at my jeans. The wind was damp, like when a rain's starting up. It brought a rotting smell from the bay.

I didn't see the woman until I was at the top of the hill—a lean figure, maybe fifty yards below me, right where the man said the grave would be. She was looking down, her arms folded across her chest, as if she was waiting for an explanation, or her turn in line. She was wearing a dark raincoat, and one of those mesh shopping bags hung from her elbow. She was old and had skinny, shapeless legs and pepper-gray hair that she must have set in pin curls. I watched her a long time. When she glanced in my direction, I looked away.

I wondered who she was, what she knew, whether she was the woman who'd written the letter to my mother. Then her whole body seemed to sigh, and she stepped away, down toward the lane on the far side of the cemetery. I walked to the grave, stood where she had stood. An arrangement of carnations, dried and brown, lay nearby. The earth of the grave was still darker than the ground around it, like Grandpa's grave. The woman had turned up the dirt in the center to plant some mums—or someone had. I knelt, touched the dirt. Fresh. The smell of the earth mixed with the sour smell of the bay. The grave marker bore the dates and a name. I held my breath. There it was. His name. Michael Mulvaney. I shivered. Miles from home, in a place as foreign and forbidding as a bad dream, I'd found the grave of someone whose connection to my mother was a cruel riddle, taunting me with how little I knew.

Yet the flowers made me feel connected to him somehow, like a witness to something private. One person, at least, had cared enough about him to say goodbye, and that made him seem less like a stranger.

I stood up, expecting to see the old woman—near the gate maybe—but she wasn't there. I felt frantic, afraid I'd lost the only link to him. I ran to the exit, breathless, almost panicky. How could the old woman have walked so fast? I wandered for a block or two, away from the cemetery into the neighborhood's colorless streets. It was a nasty day, a bleak part of Brooklyn: boarded windows, abandoned cars, graffiti in the most unlikely places. The wind took gum wrappers and McDonald's Styrofoam into circles, spinning nests of garbage and leaves into corners where kids probably gathered in darkness.

The streets seemed strange, eerie. Everything I passed was sharp-edged. Even the branches on the trees seemed too stiff, as if they had to ward off unwanted creatures. Strangest of all were the shadows—so still and dark and everywhere, a landscape of lines and squares and rigid shapes, nothing without a gray echo. The shadows blocked alleys, marked the edges of all the windows, crouched in the corners of every doorway.

Just ahead, five or six boys had staked their claim to a corner mailbox, drumming a violent rhythm against its sides. I didn't want to pass them so I turned. Onto 45th Street? 46th? I couldn't be sure. The street sign was decapitated. But there she was, the woman with the silly mesh shopping bag, coming out of a grocery store right across the street.

"Hey," I called. "Wait." She stopped, eyed me suspiciously as I rushed across the street to her.

"You're the one was in the cemetery," she said when I got close. I noticed a brogue, like my grandmother had had.

"May I talk to you?"

She sized me up with an ungentle glance.

"You knew him?" I said.

"Who?"

"Michael Mulvaney?"

"What's the difference to you?"

The woman left me there, continued up the street, but I caught up. "Do you mind talking?" I asked, but she dismissed me with a side look, kept moving at her own brisk pace, as if to say it was my business whether I talked or not. I walked beside her.

"My name is Morgan," I told her.

She paused a second, looked at me more carefully this time.

"Margaret Lindstrum's Morgan, are ya?" She seemed interested now.

"You know my mother?" I said, stopping to look at her face, but she moved on.

"Can't say I've had the pleasure."

I caught up, confused. "He knew her though, right? Mulvaney?"

The woman took a sharp breath. "Not terribly well, I don't suppose."

Several blocks went by, blocks of windowless buildings, children inexplicably joyful in their abandoned Chevys, grown-ups disheveled and weary. They made me uncomfortable. It was hard for me to imagine living like that. I felt bad for them, so poor, so without, especially the children, but mostly they scared me. I wasn't sure why. Maybe I was frightened at just how bad things could get no matter how innocent or hardworking people were. But another part of me, a part I was ashamed of, was glad that I wasn't the one who was so poor.

The woman seemed to sense my distress at how rundown everything was, the storefronts drab and bare, the buildings desperately needing repair. "Don't be thinkin' this wasn't a fine neighborhood at one time."

I said, "Hmmm," as if I understood. We came to what must have been her building, a six-story wreck of a place—different from the others only because it was still inhabited. On the stoop were three men and a young, attractive woman in a short, tight skirt. There was barely room for us to pass. As we climbed the stoop, I watched the old woman close herself in, eyes down, mesh bag clutched to her skinny chest. The foursome didn't appear to expect a greeting from her. They laughed, exchanged mocking remarks in a singsong Spanish.

"David Braverman once owned this building," the woman said when we got inside. We started up the first flight of stairs. "It was taken care of then," she said. Each time we reached a landing, the woman stopped, looked at the dirty walls or a broken banister and sighed. "The owners don't even collect the rent now." She talked between the long pauses she needed to catch her breath for the next flight. "We send it to a post office box." I heard kids yelling several floors below, then their pounding footsteps gaining on us. She braced herself, gripped the swaying banister, veins swollen on the back of her hand. The kids overtook us in a mad, wild rush of jumps and squeals and leaps and screams. "Jesus, Mary, and Joseph," she said.

The next floor was hers. 6B. I saw the tension leave the woman's face as she worked the stubborn locks to get us in. "Come into the kitchen," she said as we entered. I was glad we wouldn't have to meet under the mournful gaze of Our Lady of the Magnavox standing on the TV in the living room.

"It wasn't always like this, you know." She pulled aside the frayed lace curtain to survey the damage in the street below. "That was Kaufman's deli, right there. Now all they've got is green bananas. The smell of it. I can't go in. I tell you it breaks my heart. There's nobody left anymore."

She came away from the window, moving more slowly now, looking older than she had in the street, as if it was safe to let some of her defenses down here. She got the kettle, filled it with water, and put it on the stove, then took an old mayonnaise jar down from a yellowing metal cabinet. "We'll be needin' some tea," she said. The tea in the jar was loose and black.

"Did he know my mother a long time?"

She spooned the tea. "What's the name of your street again? In Princeton?"

"Hodge Road." Perhaps she hadn't heard me.

"How long have you been there now?"

"More than two years. Since my father joined the faculty at the university."

The woman raised her eyebrows, clearly impressed. "A fine house, no doubt."

I let her finish fussing with the tea. "How did Michael Mulvaney meet my mother?"

"I suppose it's a lovely place." She glanced toward her window again, frowned.

"Yes," I said, almost ready to give up on getting an answer. The boiling water began to rattle the kettle. I tried again. "Did he ever tell you how he knew her?"

"How?"

"How she met him?"

"Who?"

"Michael Mulvaney." I managed not to roll my eyes.

"Michael was a good man. He liked a drink, mind ya, like his father. But a good man all the same." She poured the water into a small teapot and wrapped it in a tea cozy and brought it to the table.

"I guess he told you a lot about himself?" I said.

"We talked. He knew you were living in Jersey. I understand it's quite a place you've got." As she talked she gathered up the things on the table—a pen, some mail, a small red fire truck.

"He knew who I was?"

"More rooms than a boarding house, I've heard."

"Did you say he knew where we live?" I said.

"I bet it's a mansion of a place."

"Well . . . we have plenty of room."

"Plenty." She settled herself into the chair opposite mine, as if to consider this concept. "In Derry, it was only the Protestants had plenty." A roach slipped out from behind a cabinet mounted just above us. The woman didn't see it; I pretended the same. "I know he kept in touch with your uncle Pete."

"He knew my uncle Peter?"

"Your uncle Pete. Now, there's a man who knows his mind."

"I don't understand. My uncle Peter is in San Francisco."

"And speaks it, too." She poured tea into my cup, but only enough to observe its color. Unsatisfied, she set the teapot back on the trivet.

"You know my uncle Peter?"

"Met him at the wake. I didn't see your mother there." The words sounded like an accusation.

"I guess . . . she didn't go."

"Hmm."

"Did my mother know him well?"

"Not well enough, seems to me." She was clearly annoyed now.

"This isn't bothering you, is it?" I said. "Talking about him?"

"And why would it be botherin' me?"

"I just wondered if he talked much, you know, about my mother?"

"Michael could talk the collar off a monsignor. He had a way about him, just like his father." A smile crossed her face, lighting her eyes. "Even with these godforsaken Puerto Ricans. And them not understanding a word. Just like his father."

I watched the old woman test the tea again.

"I remember one time Terence . . . "

"Terence?"

"Terence Mulvaney, Michael's father. This was before Braverman sold the building—Dave was here for the rent and I didn't have it. He liked his rent on time, Braverman. Well, wouldn't you know, Terence got him to comparing Derek Jeter to the likes of Mickey Mantle, got him so worked up he forgot what he came for." Satisfied with the color of the tea, she poured it into the cups, this time motioning for me to help myself to sugar and milk.

"But the best was when those holy rollers would come to the door, passin' out their Bible comics. A moment of your time, they'd say, and then he'd start with them, talking in tongues like he'd been touched by the Holy Spirit himself." She stirred her tea, looked toward the window, absently, taken by her memories. That bothered me, that place she had that she could go to, a way back to these people, back to the answers I wanted. I put some sugar in the tea and tasted it, expecting something really good after the way she'd fussed over it. And it was. I told her that, wanting to get her attention back.

"I have to go all the way up to the Bronx for it, near Gaelic Park, where my sister lives."

"You have a sister?"

"Catharine," she said, and the tone told me all I needed to know about how well they got along.

"Did you come to America together?"

"No. No. She's only been here ten years. Her boys came over, so she followed. Let's just say she's not adjusting well." She didn't look at me. And from the abrupt way she answered, it was clear this wasn't something she wanted to talk about. I waited a moment, no more than that.

"Do you have a picture of Michael?"

"You mean here?" Where else did she think I meant, but I didn't say it. "Well, of course, I do. Come here," she said, and rose from the table. I followed her out into the living room. She stopped in front of what seemed like a fireplace, but it was only a piece of furniture, a mantel. On it was a framed drawing of a man, done in pencil. The pose was more like a candid photo than any kind of portrait I'd ever seen. It was a close-up of his face, and he was looking back over his shoulder. He had curly hair and he glanced out from the frame with a grin that made him look as if he'd just agreed not to tell the world some outrageous news about you. He was very handsome. And there was something oddly familiar about him, about the eyes. "That's Michael Mulvaney," she said.

"He was very good looking," I said.

"Well, that was done a ways before he got sick, when he was here from Derry to visit. He came over when he could, every few years. He was a big man, six foot three, easy."

I cut her off before she could get distracted again. "Excuse me, ma'am. Did he ever tell you how he knew my mother?"

She still didn't answer me, mumbled something about finishing our tea, so I followed her back into the kitchen and sat down.

"So," I said, "what did he tell you?"

"He'd tell me what he was in a mood to tell me."

I pushed the tea away. "I think you know something and you're not telling me."

She looked at my face, examined it really. "Seems I'm not the first to be doin' that to you, child."

I thought about all the times I'd asked my mother about her childhood and got no answers. Even Grandpa and Grandma wouldn't tell me anything about it, about the family. It was as if the questions embarrassed them. Instead of answers, I got anecdotes about my mother's college years or Grandpa's life after the Vietnam War. Their life when my mother was growing up was theirs alone, something I was not supposed to bring up.

The woman seemed to be struggling with some decision. Then she sat up straight, put her cup down. "All right. It's time then. I'll show you something." She got up, and I listened to her steps as she walked to what must have been the farthest of the rooms. She returned with some photographs, placed one down in front of me.

It was an old photo, small and square. At least twenty people were crowded onto a couch in an effort to get everyone into the picture. They were seated on laps, draped across the back of the couch, squeezed together on the floor in front. I didn't recognize anyone at first. Then I looked more closely and my hands began to tremble. Practically hidden in the crowd were a dark-haired girl who looked just like me and a boy with red hair like my uncle Peter's. They were so small, so skinny. Another boy, clearly older, with hair just as red and wildly curly, sat next to the dark-haired girl. In the center of the couch, staring straight at the camera with a mischievous grin, was a huge man with broad shoulders and dark hair. A woman who had Grandma Dubrowski's nose and eyes was on one side of him; my look-alike was on the other. The girl was no more than eight. The dark-haired man had one of her long braids tucked between his nose and his upper lip.

The woman's thin, crooked finger pointed at the older of the red-haired boys. "That's Michael Mulvaney," she said. "He came home from Derry about ten years ago. He lived there since he was nineteen, with his aunt. He got involved in the Troubles. IRA. He had to come back for fear for his life."

But I already knew that was Michael Mulvaney, because I could see that the younger boy was my uncle Peter and that the girl with the braids was my mother.

I looked up at her. "He was my uncle, wasn't he?"

She nodded. "And that," she said, pointing to the big dark-haired man with the braid under his nose, "is your grandfather, Terence Mulvaney."

I felt weak, as if waves were tossing me, and it must have shown on my face, because the woman touched my hand. I had a squirrel's urge to put the photo into my bag, hoard it away to study alone, their faces, their clothes—links to a lost time, a secret past. "Michael Mulvaney gave you this?" I said.

"There's more bits of things where that came from. His things." She returned to her place at the table.

"You have them?"

"There's not much." A little of the spirit went out of her then. "They're yours if you want them," she said softly. I saw that she didn't want to part with them, these odds and ends of somebody else's life, pictures of people who were really my people, not hers. I could see that she loved him. I slid the photo across the table to her.

"And as for your grandfather. Well, there's no sort of harm in him now," the woman said, not wanting, I supposed, to speak ill of the dead. She poured herself more tea. "Still, I'm sorry for your trouble," she said.

"I'm sorry for yours, too, ma'am," I said.

"And for M&M's."

"M&M's?"

"Your mother. That was their pet name for her. M&M."

I felt dizzy, like I was on a carnival ride.

"Deirdre's my name. Deirdre Lynch. Your grandfather used to have a way of saying it that made it sound like a curse. He hated it. Christened me Clover. I met him right after I came over. He showed me the ropes."

"It's a lovely name. Did you two ever get married?"

She looked down. "I thought we might at one point, but no." Her voice trailed away.

"Clover." I repeated the name, as if to pinch myself. It had begun. The secrets were slipping away, and the sensation was eerie, off balance, like having one foot outside the real world. I put down my cup but missed the center of the saucer and spilled some tea.

"No problem, child. I'll take care of it." Clover took a small dishrag from a hook near the sink and wiped the table. "I suppose you have people to take care of this kind of thing at home. There must be no end to the chores when you have so much company," she said.

"Company?"

"At that grand house of yours."

"No. Not really. Once in a while."

"Pity. The waste."

"Waste?"

"Lovely guest rooms in a lovely house and no guests in them."

"We have guests now and then," I said, although that wasn't really true anymore. My parents were never home long enough to have people sleep over.

"I see." She handed me the photograph, meaning for me to have it along with the others.

"Oh, no," I said. "That's all right. You keep them. Maybe I could just have a look at them again someday."

"You're always welcome here," she said, smiling, then poured me more of the tea, as if we'd done this before, as if she knew without asking that I'd want more.

three

The trip back to Princeton took a long time. My train was delayed just after it left Penn Station, and I sat looking out into the darkness of the tunnel. My face was reflected in the glass, but I wasn't sure anymore who was looking back at me. It was like spotting someone you think you know, but it turns out to be a stranger. In my hand was the photo Clover had slipped into my coat pocket as I was leaving. I had found it when I got on the train.

When I arrived at the station, I got on my bike and headed for the library, but my friend Sarah wasn't there. Neither was Ansel. So I went to Sarah's house. I rang her doorbell just once, then pedaled back up the long brick driveway to a spot by the road where I knew she could see me from her window. I wasn't in the mood for Mrs. Richardson's play-by-play of her latest purchases and her less-than-subtle critiques of my taste in clothes. She was an art dealer, and she treated everyone like a canvas she had to assess.

The door opened and Sarah waved to me. She practically skipped down the wide front steps, then hiked up her long linen skirt to get on her bike. Long skirts were hardly what most Princeton High School girls were wearing. But most Princeton girls didn't shop in flea markets and Goodwill stores, searching for odd shirts, oversized jackets, and baggy trousers. Sarah had taken to wearing no-name sneakers that she bought at Walmart and accessories from Army surplus. She'd become a source of anguish to her mother, a woman who took comfort from labels and felt cheated that she'd been born into a generation that was forced to wear them inside their garments. Sarah's bohemian look was only a few weeks old, and I doubted she'd stay away from the designer racks any longer than it took to get her mother to increase her clothing allowance, which was what the seedy togs were really all about. Sarah's affection for expensive things ran deep. Her iPod had a Versace leather case.

I liked Sarah a lot. She was a good friend. She was sixteen like me, but the frail type, blonde. Her looks were the opposite of mine. So was her temperament. I was dark and sturdy, and until I came to Princeton, I didn't make fashion statements, funky or otherwise. The truth was I didn't care all that much what I wore.

As Sarah got closer, I busied myself with my pocketbook so she wouldn't see the look on my face, but she already sensed that something was up. "What's wrong?" she said. I shook my head in a way that said, "Not now." I didn't want to tell her about Clover, not yet. I wasn't really sure what she'd make of my having relatives—even dead ones—in a place as rundown as Clover's neighborhood.

"I thought we were supposed to go to the library after school? You weren't there," I said, and for some reason my voice cracked. It was silly, but when I didn't find them there, I'd felt lost, the way I did at home. I thought about my mother whispering on the phone, about taking a job in the Chicago office again. She never talked about it openly, at least not to me. But I wasn't going back there. I wasn't moving again, not ever, and not there.

"We didn't think you'd be going. When you weren't in school today, we figured you were taking another day off. You know." They thought I was upset about my grandfather. At the funeral, I'd told them I'd be back in school the next day. They knew nothing about Brooklyn.

I shrugged. "I just wasn't feeling good this morning," I said. She nodded, as if she understood. "I'm fine now."

"I was going to the mall. Want to come?"

"Not really."

She sighed. "It's okay. It's a drag to go there on bikes anyway. Maybe I can talk my mother into taking us later in the week. It's easier with the car. And if I tell her I'm ready to return to Nordstrom, she'll probably agree to carry us on her back."

I smiled, but it was a weak one.

"Want to come in and hang out for a while? You've got to hear what Kathy Beckham told us last night." Sarah had that look in her eye, a cross between shock and delight, which usually meant she was about to share a play-by-play on the blow job somebody had just awarded another undeserving thrill seeker. I didn't want to hear about it, but Sarah's fascination with the whole business was limitless. She'd never done it herself. I played dumb. I hadn't told her it wasn't a whole lot of fun. Sometimes I could still feel the rough boards of Mike's sun porch under my knees, his hands in my hair. I'd thought he'd want to be with me after that. He did, but never as a real date, only for that. But I'd felt so alone in Chicago, and I'd convinced myself that having him that way was better than nothing.

"What do you want to do then?" said Sarah.

"I want to go to the library. We were supposed to meet Ansel there at three o'clock, weren't we?"

"Are you sure you're up for that?" Sarah seemed to think I needed R&R more than schoolwork.

"We need to get some work done, yes." Schoolwork was the last thing I wanted to do. I could barely think straight, but I wanted to talk to Ansel. "The report is a big piece of our history grade."

"Okay. Let's go get him," Sarah said. "He's at Mr. Kinsey's store."

Mr. Kinsey was an old friend of Ansel's parents. Very old. So old he had a lot of trouble taking care of his stationery store, so Ansel's parents encouraged him to help the old man when he had deliveries or when his arthritis was acting up. His parents got their jollies off doing things like that. They had major money, but they didn't want to spend any of it, not even on charities, so they looked for funky ways to give back to the universe. Their favorite projects were the ones they could assign to Ansel.

Kinsey's Stationers had been on Nassau Street for more than seventy years. Mr. Kinsey had been running it since his father retired in 1976. None of Mr. Kinsey's three sons was interested in doing the same, so he was on his own now. He had an apartment upstairs above the store, but he couldn't manage the stairs anymore, so he lived in the rooms in the back. He was comfortable there. He had a kitchen and a dog with broad shoulders and short legs. Ansel called the dog Secret Service because he treated old Kinsey like he was the president. When people didn't keep their distance, he growled politely, as if wanting to make his point without upsetting any voters.

Mr. Kinsey looked up from his work when he heard the entrance bell. "Mr. Fagan's in the storeroom," he said to us. Mr. Kinsey was used to our visits when Ansel was at the store. "He's all yours. I'll be closing up in a jiffy." Mr. Kinsey talked as if he could still move like a twenty-year-old, saying things like "right away" or "this will just take a minute." Most things took him a lot longer than that, if he could manage them at all.

Back in the storeroom, Ansel was standing on a step stool, stocking shelves. He was wearing the same kind of thing he'd wear to school: cut-off jeans, a T-shirt, and the pin-striped vest of a Caraceni suit his father had relegated to the pile of clothes headed for the consignment shop. His Phillies cap was turned around, and his sandy blond hair was pressed under it, except for a handful that poked out rooster-like through the hole in the back of the cap. Ansel Fagan was an average-looking kid, average height, average build, the kind who gets lost in a crowd. You'd never figure him for the one who hung the condom on the bulletin board with the lost-and-found notices, the one who had a photo of the football team on his Facebook page, their heads replaced by those of *Sesame Street* characters.

"What's going on? You weren't in school today. We were supposed to go to the library," Ansel whined. He had a way of making Sarah and me feel we'd neglected him, although the ploy wasn't as effective as it was when we first became friends. A month earlier, Sarah and I had gone to a tarot card reading and didn't invite him along. The reading was Sarah's idea, an attempt to lift my spirits. She was trying to shake me out of the moods I'd fallen into after my grandfather got so sick. Most of the crazier things Sarah and I did were her idea: the Popeye tattoos, the astrological diet-plan charts, the self-administered acupuncture to cure split ends. Sarah was a child of the occult, a seeker of truth—any kind that would spice up an ordinary day. I didn't mind the everyday that much. I preferred the expected, liked to be able to count on people. Maybe that was because my mother's whereabouts from week to week were anybody's guess. Atlanta. Chicago. Dallas. I was never sure where she'd be or for how long. My father taught astrophysics and did research, so he was around more often. At least he appeared to be around. His head was mostly in the stars and his nose in a book.

"I'm surprised to find you here," said Sarah. "I thought maybe you'd be going to the game with Twinkle Poms."

"Come on," Ansel said. "Susan's got her good points." Susan was Ansel's new girlfriend, something I didn't like to think about.

"You mean besides the two that got you interested in the first place?" Sarah said.

Ansel laughed, got down from the stool, and plopped himself on a crate. Sarah and I pulled up crates of our own. "I've got to get out of this deal," Ansel told us for the umpteenth time. "He's been working me like a dog." We nodded sympathetically, even though we knew Ansel's capacity for physical labor was much more akin to a cat's.

Ansel leaned forward, sank his head into his palms, and went on with his sad story. I knew all of Ansel's stories. We were close, had been since I fell crazy in love with him, which happened the first time he spoke to me the first day we met two years before, at the start of freshman year. He liked to pretend he always knew what I was thinking, but, of course, he didn't. I had never given Ansel even the tiniest clue about how I felt.

In any case, Ansel didn't think of me as someone to date. I didn't blame him, really. I didn't have much to brag about in the way of looks. Sarah tried to convince me that wasn't true. Easy for her to say. She was everything every girl wants to be, delicate and petite. I looked like an egghead on steroids. I was nearly as tall as my father, almost five-ten. Sarah liked to put a better spin on it, saying I had an athlete's figure and that people admired my hazel eyes. Ansel said he couldn't understand why my eyes weren't brown, said they didn't match my dark lashes and dark brown hair. And he'd told me early on I ought to lose the bulky shirts. At least he didn't sugarcoat it.

The day I met Ansel was my first day in yet another new school. We had just moved to Princeton, where my father would be teaching at the university. Before that, he spent two years at the University of Chicago, and before that, Stanford. We never stayed long, but it was long enough to finally make a few friends, long enough for losing them to hurt. Ansel's locker was next to mine, and I was having trouble with the lock the office had loaned me, so he offered to help. I gave him the combination, and he had it open in seconds. He called me his damsel in distress, and I pretended not to like it. Then I saw the photo taped to the inside of his locker door—a blonde chic type, contagious smile, obviously accustomed to adoration— and I knew there was no hope for me. Had I looked more closely, the layers of old tape might have tipped me off that the thing with the blonde wouldn't last long, but by the time it ended, I'd gotten really good at hiding how I felt. Ansel told me all his troubles—especially his girl troubles—and before long he seemed to me just like a girlfriend, closer than a brother. That was better than nothing.

Ansel thought I didn't know much about sex, at least not in practice. I guess because Sarah was such a babe in the woods, he assumed I was, too. Sarah talked about her inexperience like it was a badge of honor. I didn't talk about that stuff at all—or really much of anything that I'd done in Chicago. Nobody needed to know. But I wondered sometimes if I'd have had a better chance with Ansel if he knew. I was pretty sure he was having some kind of sex with Twinkle Poms. But he was more relaxed around Sarah and me. He got to act like the experienced guy, older and wiser—by all of three months.

I loved being with Ansel—even when he was complaining. His silliness made almost any problem seem pointless to worry about. Even now, my trip to Brooklyn that morning began to seem distant.

"Well, come on," Sarah said to Ansel. "Let's hit the stacks."

"I can't. The old man will think I'm a shirker. He'll never believe I have school work to do."

"So tell him Twinkle Poms needs you to lift her spirits," said Sarah.

Ansel gave her a look but managed to charm his way past Mr. Kinsey with a flurry of urgent excuses and slippery promises to return the next day. We doubted it.

The library had just enough stray scholars to draw Ansel and me be-quiet looks from the librarian. Sarah had finally left us alone at the table and went to search the database. Right away, Ansel asked what was wrong. "It's my mother," I said.

"What about her?"

"She's been lying to me," I said, too upset to keep my voice down.

Ansel stood *Immigrants to America* up on its binding to shield us from the librarian's gaze and scraped his heavy chair closer to mine. "So what else is new?" he whispered. "Don't parents specialize in hiding stuff?" Ansel's mother hadn't got around to telling him how sick his grandmother really was until they were selling the old woman's furniture and finding her a nursing home.

"This is different," I said.

"What do you mean?"

"I heard my parents talking the other night, the night before my grandfather's funeral. My mom was blaming herself for not being able to give him a kidney."

"Shush," the librarian told us.

Ansel leaned closer. "You've got to expect that. She's probably going to go on like that for a long while. She's upset."

"It's not just that. My father kept telling her it wasn't her fault. Why would he have to say that if it were just about her blood type?"

"Ask them."

"I asked them the next morning."

"So what did they say?"

My laugh came out like a snort. "She told me I'd heard them wrong."

Ansel rolled his eyes. "Oh, man," he said.

"They're not going to tell me anything." I didn't mention that there was now an even longer list of questions I didn't have answers to, like how long it would be before my mom moved us back to Chicago, or why she'd been pretending for years that Grandpa was her real father.

"Why should you be any different from the rest of us?" He leaned forward, about to say more, but changed his mind and backed away.

"What is it? What were you going to say?"

He hesitated, just a heartbeat, then leaned toward me again. "Today my dad got a phone call at two in the morning. At breakfast, he tells my mom it was one of his hedge-fund managers in Asia." I rolled my eyes. Ansel chuckled. "And she believed him."

I wanted to tell Ansel where I had been that morning, but I couldn't say it. "My mother treats me like I don't matter, like I have no need to know anything."

Ansel knew what things had been like for me at home ever since Chicago: My parents' long, urgent discussions behind closed doors, the even-longer silences that followed, my failed attempts to get anyone, even Grandpa, to tell me what was wrong. "But this is different," he said. "You have a right to expect some answers."

"I'm getting my own answers. I'm not waiting around for her to tell me anything."

Sarah came to the table and dropped a stack of books with a soft but annoying thud. "Are you guys working or yakking?"

"Sarah, chill out," said Ansel. "We've got until Thanksgiving to finish this thing."

The thing was a team history assignment—an independent study on a current national issue. Each team had until mid-November to choose a topic—some problem in American society—find out how it started and what was being done about it, then draw some conclusions about what was likely to happen in the future.

Sarah, Ansel, and I had formed a team. That was the easy part. We were already a team. The hard part was getting the work done. We'd chosen homelessness as our topic, mostly because nobody else had proposed it, and by the time we got around to submitting one, the stuff we really wanted was taken. Sarah suggested we do something on how the women's movement affected corporate America, but Ansel said that was old news. He wanted to do the paper on how financial markets influence American policy making, but Mr. Marcus already had papers on that. I just wanted it over with, but in the end I was the one who came up with the topic: Homelessness in the Land of Plenty. It was an expression my grandfather used when he was lamenting how the country had gone wrong.

"Look," Sarah whispered at us, "I found something that compares the number of homeless in the sixties to the numbers since 2000."

"Good work, Sarah," Ansel said. "Go for it."

"Can I get some help on this?" She slid a thick, faded gray volume to our side.

I pushed it away. "I can't deal with this right now."

"You okay?" she said. I could see she felt sorry for me. She must have figured I was thinking about my grandfather.

I shrugged. "I'm fine."

"You still playing tomorrow?" She was talking about our playoff game, but for a second, I didn't know what she meant.

"Yeah, I'll be there."

She smiled, I bet partly because the team needed me as goalie. "Are you going on the bus, or is your mother taking you?"

"My mother's not going." Sarah didn't say anything. My mother missing games was nothing new, but I could see Sarah was surprised she wouldn't be at this one. "She's going to Chicago."

"Well, my mom's probably going to drive me. You can come with us if you want."

I nodded, and Sarah returned to the shelves.

"What else is going on?" Ansel said. He knew there had to be more to the story.

I looked at the floor instead of at him. "I found a letter," I said, "a note really." My voice was mostly a whisper.

"What did you say?" said Ansel. "I can't hear you."

"I said I found a note. It was addressed to my mother. It was about someone who died, someone named Michael Mulvaney. It was in pieces, and she must have taped it back together."

"Where did you find it?"

"In her briefcase."

"What else did it say?"

"It mentioned someone named M&M. Something about this guy Mulvaney asking for M&M at the end."

"Well, if she tore it up, it can't mean that much to her," he said.

"Ansel, she held onto it, kept it in her briefcase. I know she's hiding something."

"I'm not sure I'd call it hiding. It's not like she had it under her mattress. It's her briefcase."

"Listen to me. I found the woman who wrote the letter. I know who she is."

"How do you know? Who is she?"

"She's in Brooklyn."

"You went to Brooklyn?"

"Yes. And I know who Mulvaney was, and I know my mother has been lying to me. She's been lying to me all my life."

"Morgan—"

Sarah was heading toward the table. "I don't want Sarah to know about this." I could see he didn't understand why. "I need you to keep this between us."

"Morgan, what's going on? What happened in Brooklyn?"

"Not now."

I took two books from the top of the pile, opened one up, but I couldn't do it. I couldn't focus. Ansel was right. I had a right to some answers. I pushed my chair back as quietly as I could. Sarah stared at me, puzzled. "I'm sorry," I told her. "I have to go."

four

I found my mother in her room, getting ready for her trip to Chicago. She'd be there for more than a week. She had a trade show and client presentations back to back. Clothes and shoes were littered here and there, considered and cast aside. The overnight case on the bed was just about full. Her preparations had reached their final stage. Her flight left at eight in the morning, which meant she'd be ready to leave for the airport before the night was over. Mom always left on time.

"Where have you been? Did you have practice after school?" Mom said. She held up a plum-colored wool suit by its hanger. Another suit lay on the bed. My mom looked purposeful, in a hurry but not frenzied. She spoke without looking at me. "You had a call from Ansel just a few minutes ago. He said you didn't answer your cell. Louisa had to go, but she said to tell you she put your jeans in the dryer. Don't leave them in there too long or they'll wrinkle." She lifted a gray suit from the bed, held it next to the purple, and for the moment the gray seemed to have the edge. "Do you have plans for dinner? I think Dad wants to take you out. I can't go. Liz and Joan will be here soon. I have to meet with the planning committee. Liz has completely dropped the ball on the flowers." She glanced at me to see if I was getting any of this. "Turns out she never confirmed the order."

I moved into the room without answering her chatter, headed for the chair in the corner. A black silk blouse was draped over the back of it, and I sat lightly on the chair's expensive peach fabric. I held the photo Clover had given me.

My mom tossed the double-breasted gray back onto the bed. "There's a button missing," she complained. "Anyway, I think I wore that the last time." Her mind was already on Chicago, filling up with her answers to other people's problems: their budgets, their strategies, their cost-effective solutions.

"Why do you have to go?" I said.

"I told you. We have no flowers for the gala. We have to figure something out. We have two senators and a governor—not to mention the CEO of Biotech—coming, and the place is going to look like a barn."

"I mean Chicago. Why do you have to go to Chicago?"

"Morgan, we have a huge account on the hook," she said, puzzled that I was asking. "We have to prepare the presentation. I told you all this."

I slid my fingertip along the edges of the photo for the thousandth time, wondering how my mother would dodge the questions this time. I straightened my shoulders, took one more deep breath. "I want to know about Terence Mulvaney," I said.

Mom looked at me and, almost as quickly, looked away, rattled, desperate for a reason not to answer me. She put down the suit, moved a strand of hair from her face, struggled to compose herself, to continue with the packing, but her hands were trembling, her face flushed. "I wore the purple the last time I was in Chicago. I'm sure of it," she muttered, and walked back into her closet to put it away.

I wasn't going to let her stonewall me again. "I want to know about Terence Mulvaney," I called to her.

The hangers stopped scraping along the pole, and my mother appeared in the doorway. "Who gave you that name?"

"It doesn't matter." I considered telling her that I'd had to search her room like someone starving for scraps she might leave around.

"Answer me," she said. Her voice sounded fragile, as if it might crack. "Who?"

"Clover." I watched her face. I wanted the name to hurt her. I wanted it to crack open her stash of secrets, leave her exposed.

Mom closed her eyes tightly, as if she'd just taken a blow. She pinched the bridge of her nose and let her head fall slightly forward.

"How did she find you?"

"It doesn't matter." Because I knew the question was about her, not me. She didn't want any contact with Clover. That much was clear.

My mom took a breath and swallowed hard. "That's right," she said finally. Her voice was calm, the kind of voice she used on the phone to people who worked for her, people who required instructions. "And Terence Mulvaney doesn't matter, doesn't make one bit of difference. Not in my life or yours."

"I want to know why you've kept him a secret."

"No, you don't," she said, and went back into the closet.

When she turned away, I was so angry I wanted to throw something. "Your brother Michael is dead," I said. "But you already know that."

There was no response, not until she appeared in the doorway again, her face hollow and closed. "Yes," she said. "I know."

"I want to know about Terence Mulvaney," I said, getting to my feet.

"No, you don't," she said. "Believe me."

The words were like a slap. She'd been picking and choosing what I was allowed to know about her, as if I were some lackey on her staff. "Believe *you*? What a joke."

"Morgan, don't do this."

"I want to know."

Mom stood up straighter, came around to my side of the bed. "All right then," she said, motioning for me to sit back down.

"I'll tell you everything you need to know." She sat on the bed, folded her hands neatly on her lap, looked straight into my eyes. Her anger made her face rigid. "Terence Mulvaney was a worthless man who brought pain to everyone in his life."

"He was . . . he was your father," I said.

She looked down, as if that fact made it hard for her to face anyone, even her own daughter. "Yes, my father, but . . . " She swallowed hard, continued in a harsh whisper, determined to be done with this. "He was my father, but he didn't know how to be one; he knew even less about being a husband." She stood, put a hand through her thick, dark hair, and looked down at me. "Morgan, the less you know about Terence Mulvaney, the better off you'll be," she said, her voice steady now, reasonable.

She moved purposefully around to the other side of the room and returned to her packing, gathering up hangers from the bed, as if the matter was settled and there was nothing more to say. I'd been dismissed. I didn't count. Nothing I felt about any of this could matter.

I stood up. "That's up to me," I said. "Isn't that up to me?"

Mom gave me a hard look. "Frankly, Morgan, it isn't. I crossed him out of my life sixteen years ago," she said, pointing a hanger at me, "and he's not getting back in."

"What about my life? I want to know who's real and who isn't."

She unzipped the garment bag, a shrill sound like she was sharpening a knife. "My grandfather was a phony," I said, refusing to be ignored. "Some stranger I've never heard of turns out to be your father. Who's the girl in this picture?" I held out the photo. "It's you, isn't it? Don't you want to see this?" I moved closer to her. "Who are these people? Tell me."

Mom moved several steps away from me, as if the photo might harm her if she didn't keep her distance. "No, I don't want to see it," she told me, but I kept coming. She pushed my hand away and the photo fluttered toward the carpet like a dying leaf. Rushing to get it, I started to cry.

"Morgan, I'm sorry. Please come sit down." She pushed her suits aside, so we could sit on her bed.

"I needed to protect you," she said, sitting close, her arm around me.

"You're protecting yourself, not me."

"Your grandfather and your uncle were not the type of people you needed to know about."

"Why? Because they made you unhappy?" It was obvious I had no place in her drama. It was entirely about her and how to keep things the way she wanted them.

"That's not the point. I'm talking about criminal activity."

"Criminal activity?" I couldn't believe it. It didn't fit anything Clover had said. A nice old woman like Clover wouldn't be around anyone like that.

She could see I didn't believe her. "My brother was a member of the IRA," she said, lowering her voice.

"The Irish Republican Army?" My mind filled with images of armed men, their faces covered in dark woolen masks.

"Yes, and I'm not talking about a romantic band of freedom fighters. I'm talking about thugs who killed and maimed innocent people and undermined any chance for peace that country had."

"You mean he killed people?"

"He helped them do it and that's the same thing."

"What about your father? Was he involved, too?"

She looked up. My father was standing in the doorway. "What's wrong?" he said, as if he'd wandered into some unfamiliar galaxy.

"John," she said. And something relaxed in her, as if now that my father was there, she was free to drop the subject. "Just some girl talk," she told him.

"Liz and Joan are here," Dad said, and turned away, no doubt relieved not to have to hear any more than that.

"We'll talk some more, Morgan," Mom said. "Everything will be all right."

I just sat there, but she got up.

"Be a dear and tell Joan and Liz I'll be right down. I'm nearly done here." She made a big deal of nestling the gray suit snugly into the bag. When I didn't answer, she looked at me. "I'll call you from Chicago," she said, as if that would be enough.

I waited until after my mother left for her meeting, then went to my dad's study, listened outside the door. Bach. Good. A sign that he was nibbling on some stray inspirations and not in the throes of unraveling the secrets of space, for which he required alternating doses of complete silence and ear-splitting tracks from Black Sabbath. I tapped softly. "Dad?"

"Morgan, is that you?" he said. "Come in."

He was seated at his desk, a pale wiry man, lost behind mountains of books—piles of them, stacks, opened, closed, cast aside, waiting their turn. A large crystal ashtray on the windowsill behind him overflowed with cigarette butts of assorted lengths and brands, and smoke hung in the sunlight around him, making his pale face all the more unearthly. "Morgan," he said, smiling, "come here." He hurried to put out his cigarette and held his arms out to me. I saw the look on his face, as if I'd caught him in the midst of something sinful. Enjoying his research so much embarrassed him.

I gave him a quick hug, cleared some books away, and found a spot on his couch. He offered to turn off the music, but I told him there was no need.

"So tell me what's happened," he said. "Your mother's not being clear."

"I . . . I found a letter," I began. He looked concerned. "A letter that was addressed to Mom." I could see he was lost. "It was in her briefcase."

"I see," he said.

He didn't, but I went on. "It mentioned people I never heard of." I hesitated. Dad waited. "Someone named M&M," I said, and watched his face. Sure enough, his expression changed, as if he were struggling to retrieve some memory from his crowded gray matter, something he wasn't sure he knew. "It was signed by someone named Clover, telling her that a man named Michael Mulvaney had died."

Dad looked away, avoiding my eyes, and I saw this was going to be hard for him. He shifted in his chair, patted the front of his jacket, trying unsuccessfully to locate his Winstons. Their absence distressed him more than usual, and he began searching—a little frantic—among the books on his desk for the hidden pack. I'd seen these attacks before. His desperation was contagious. I stood and joined him behind the desk to help him find the cigarettes. I spotted them on the windowsill behind him. "Here, Dad."

"You're an angel," he said, and teased a cigarette out of the pack. "So you must tell me, Morgan. Are things improving for you at school?" He picked up a shiny gold lighter, snapped it open, and lit the cigarette. The first drag worked to calm him. "Are you making progress on that term paper?"

"Dad?"

"It's an intriguing topic you've chosen. The question of our obligation to the less fortunate predates recorded history. Did you know that? Even the Neanderthals cared for the needy."

"That's not—"

"Archaeologists have unearthed the fossil remains of people with physical disabilities that would have prevented them from surviving on their own. Rather than abandoning their handicapped brethren, early man chose to protect them."

"Dad?" I said, and touched his hand. He surrendered then, let me ask the question. "Did you know Michael Mulvaney?"

He coughed, a lengthy, loud series of explosions that aborted each effort to answer. "Can't . . . " he finally caught his breath and blurted, "Can't say I ever met the man."

I patted him on the back to relieve his coughing and his embarrassment. "Okay, Dad," I said. Maybe it was tough for a scientist to play games with the truth. I sat back down on the couch. "I went to Brooklyn today," I told him without ceremony. "I met Clover."

He came and sat beside me, took a slow, deep drag to gather strength. "How much do you know?" he said, getting right to the point. There was no way to ease into it.

"That Grandpa was not my real grandfather. That this Terence Mulvaney was Mom's real father." I showed him the picture, told him about Clover.

"How did you manage to find her?"

"Actually, I found *him*. His grave."

"You mean Michael Mulvaney's?"

"Yes. I figured he probably lived in Brooklyn, and I knew he was dead. Churches are in charge of dead people, so I started calling some. I got some answers on the third call, from a secretary at the rectory at St. Frances de Chantal Parish. That was his parish. She knew him."

Dad waited for more. I could see he was impressed.

"The woman told me other stuff, too. He was born in New York but lived in Ireland for many years. Came back to America about ten years ago. He died in early September, barely a month ago; it was fresh in her mind. He was only fifty-two, but he'd been sick for a while. She seemed sad about it. She wasn't allowed to give an address over the phone, but she was willing to confirm that he was buried in Green-Wood Cemetery. Then I called the cemetery and the man I talked to told me where the grave was."

He held the picture at arm's length, far enough to see, even without his glasses, that the young girl with the braids was clearly Mom. He held on to the photo awkwardly, not sure what to do next. "Well then," he began, squinting into the cigarette smoke. "What the woman said was true." He cleared his throat in an official kind of way. "Yes," he said, using his glasses to see the photo this time, "that must be him, your mother's father, right there." He pointed to the big dark-haired man. He got quiet, maybe hoping somehow that that would cover it, but the look on my face told him that we were not done yet. "He was not, I suppose, what anyone would call a model parent in any respect," he went on, handing me back the photo. He pulled on the cigarette, and the tip glowed. He held the smoke in a heartbeat longer before exhaling. "Spent a good deal of time drinking, I'm afraid. Grandma finally left him when your mother was eleven."

It was so strange to hear these things. It didn't feel as if they were really about us, about our family. I'd been shut out of everything for so long that my father could have been telling me about the people down the street, about virtual strangers. "What else did Mom tell you about it?" I said.

"She really hasn't talked about it much." Dad started looking about, and I realized he needed his ashtray. I fetched it from the windowsill for him. The coffee table was covered with more papers and books, but I found a place for the ashtray. "Most of this I got from Grandpa and your uncle Peter. Your mother doesn't talk about it."

It hurt to know that Grandpa had held all this back from me. "Why did everyone pretend? Why did this all have to be a secret?" But I knew at least part of the answer. My mom was Grandpa's princess. He never would have said anything against her wishes.

Dad put the cigarette out. "Your mother insisted. Your grandparents agreed." He took out the crumpled pack for another cigarette. "Grandpa didn't like it, but it wasn't up to him."

"But why did she want to pretend?"

My dad sighed. "Michael was in the IRA. Your mother felt he had become a criminal. She didn't want to be in contact with him, didn't want you to be exposed to that kind of fanatical ideology. And, of course, she wanted nothing to do with her father."

"But she told *you* about him?"

He hesitated then, shook his head. "Grandpa told me, many years ago." He looked so lonely saying this. "I've talked to her, of course, about telling you, but she was immovable. It's been terribly difficult for me, Morgan. I want you to understand that. I have never approved of keeping this from you."

"But what good does hiding it do? Hiding him from me?"

"Maybe she thinks she can erase him. At eleven, she was old enough to know what a family was supposed to be." I nodded, to show him I understood, but really I didn't. And I couldn't help wondering if she would have felt differently if her father hadn't been so poor. "Tell me more about this Clover woman. You showed remarkable ingenuity in finding her, I must say. What's she like?"

I wasn't going to answer his questions. If he wanted to know what Clover was like, he could go find out for himself. If they'd had their way, she'd still be a secret, someone they were ashamed of, just like Terence and Michael Mulvaney. When I didn't respond, he put out his cigarette, then rose from the couch, clearly eager to have an end to this. "Let me take you out to dinner. You can tell me all about how your paper is coming along."

I got up. I wanted it over with, too. "The paper's fine. I have to go."

"Morgan, I'm sorry about this," he said.

"Yeah," I said, opening the door. Then I remembered my game, but I don't know why I bothered asking him about it. I could have scripted his answer. "Are you coming to the game tomorrow?"

"The game?"

"We're in the playoffs."

"Oh, your soccer team. Of course. So you've had a good season?"

"Yeah, Dad. We had a good season," I told him, and left before he could say something even more clueless.

five

Just outside of Princeton, set way back from the road, there was an old Quaker meeting house built in the early eighteenth century. Beside it was a cemetery, just as old, tucked in on all four sides by a low stone wall that Ansel, Sarah, and I used to take in a hop if we had to. But we rarely did, because the little black gate was always open and we could slip inside easily. On nights when the Friends met—that's what the Quakers call themselves—we were careful not to disturb the place.

But on most nights there was no one around, and we could rest our backs against the wall's southeast corner where we could see the moon rise and sit eye level with the finely chiseled gravestone of Mrs. R. Nelson Peabody, who'd been placed there shortly after August 18, 1868. As far as we could tell from the headstone, Mr. Peabody never joined her there. We speculated sometimes on what became of him. Ansel thought he died in the Civil War or ran away and got buried at sea. Sarah figured he was under there somewhere but the church forgot to mention it on the stone. But I always suspected that he left Mrs. R. to spend his last years with someone else. I wondered how my parents' last years would be. Would they even be together?

That night wasn't the first time I'd come to the cemetery alone. Sometimes Grandpa would moan when his pain meds didn't work so well, and I couldn't stand it, couldn't stand not being able to do anything for him. Now I was angry at him, which I knew was ridiculous. He was gone. But he had been lying, too. He could have told me. And now he wasn't there to help me with any of it. I didn't know who I was anymore, who I could believe.

The moon was the cemetery's only light, and I was glad it was full. I opened the squeaky gate and sat down by the wall, watched the leaves lit by the moon. They skipped and swirled from grave to grave, hurrying to pay their random respects. I heard a sound and glanced toward the lane beyond the gate. It was Ansel, and he wasn't alone. Two ghostly shadows swayed on bikes. The second was Sarah. Seeing them made me lightheaded. I thought of getting back on my bike. I wanted to be alone. I wasn't sure what I should tell them about all this, about Mulvaney, especially Sarah. What would she make of it? What would she make of me, with a poverty-stricken Irish immigrant for a grandfather. She'd freak out. I was sure of it.

"Why aren't you answering your phone?" Ansel said. He looked worried. "Did your mother tell you I called the house?"

"Are you okay?" Sarah said. "What's going on?" I didn't answer. "Will somebody please tell me what's wrong?"

I realized then that Ansel hadn't told her much. "Okay," I said. But you'd better brace yourself." They both sat down, and I leaned back against the wall. The words came out in a burst of anger and confusion. Halfway through, I stopped to catch my breath. I described how Clover had put the photo on the table in front of me, how my mother wouldn't even look at it. I gulped down another breath as I showed it to them, thought about stopping before I got to the part about Mulvaney's drinking, but I managed to tell them the rest. Still, the rush of fear came back, the fear of more awful secrets waiting to surface— and I was afraid I was going to cry. Ansel and Sarah could tell. Sarah looked away, and Ansel offered some gum. Nobody knew what to say. We got up, walked through the tiny cemetery, read the names on the stones, all familiar by then.

"You look awful," said Ansel.

"She's upset," said Sarah. "Who wouldn't be?" It was as if she didn't want me to say any more about it. I could see it made her uncomfortable.

"At least now you know what the letter was about," said Sarah. "You know why she kept her father a secret."

"I don't get it really," said Ansel. "Okay, so he drank and your grandmother divorced him. Is that really something you need to hide from your daughter for years and years?"

"It is if you're ashamed of it," said Sarah.

"But what was there to hide? He was out of the picture," said Ansel. "I mean it wasn't as if he was beating down the door to bounce Morgan on his knee." This hadn't occurred to me before, but it hit me now like a slap.

"Yeah. What kind of man doesn't want to see his grandchild?" said Sarah. "Maybe your mother was right to do what she did."

"Right to make their lives a masquerade?" said Ansel.

Sarah hesitated. "Why not? Some people are in our lives whether we like it or not. We're stuck with them. But there's no law that says we have to like it. And if we can do something about it, why not? I think your mother did the right thing."

"It isn't about right or wrong," said Ansel. "Ignoring something doesn't end it."

"It did as far as she's concerned," I said.

"I don't believe that," Ansel said. "Listen. I know this isn't the same thing, but when my brother was born, I knew there was something wrong with him. But that's all I knew." I'd heard Ansel talk about his younger brother before, how he was "put away" when he was very little, and the story always reminded me that there was more to Ansel than the clown mask he wore so often. "My parents never talk about him. They never talk about where he is or how he is. 'He was severely retarded,' they'll say, as if that explains everything. Meanwhile, they never look each other in the eye, and if we have to spend more than five minutes together, we have to make sure there's a TV on because the silence is lethal." Ansel tossed a rock against a tree. I watched the muscles in his jaw tense. The hurt settled into the corners of his eyes. "Hiding something doesn't make it go away. It's like living on eggshells." Ansel lowered his voice, glanced at me. "That's what your mother's been doing, worrying about anybody finding out, especially you, and trying to pretend she isn't angry and hurt."

"But you can't blame her," Sarah said. "I'd be ashamed of him, too."

I looked at Sarah, but it was too late for her to take it back. I was surprised how much it hurt to hear it out loud. That was what I'd been fearing most, from the moment I saw the photograph and realized that my real grandfather had to be hidden, that Grandpa Dubrowski was a coverup for something ugly, something wrong in my family and maybe even wrong in me.

Sarah caught the look on my face. "I didn't mean it like that," she insisted. "I was just trying to see things from your mom's point of view."

"It's okay. Forget it," I said.

"Really, Morgan. I don't care if your grandfather was in al-Qaeda. It doesn't change how I feel about you."

"I know," I said, trying to believe that was true.

"Listen," Ansel said, "if you want to talk about this some more . . ."

"I don't want to talk. There's no point in talking. My parents will just keep bullshitting me."

"He means if you're upset," said Sarah.

"I know what he means. I don't want to talk. I want to do something. I want to find out who the hell my family really was." They didn't understand what I was saying, so I just came out with it. "Will you come to Brooklyn with me?"

"Brooklyn?" said Sarah. She sounded as if I'd just asked her to wander into Tehran wearing a tank top and Bodi pants.

"I want to talk to Clover again. I want some answers."

"I don't know," said Ansel. "Is that really a good idea?"

I could see they wanted no part of it. We came to the gate again; the wind was busy in the trees. "I've got to go," Sarah said. "My father's in town tonight." Mr. Richardson was a real estate developer. He was on the road a lot. When he was home, he seemed to think that enforcing every rule made up for all the time he spent away. Ansel and I followed Sarah out of the cemetery gate. The bikes were waiting near the little dirt road. The night sky was wide and bright, the trees noisy and bending close around us.

Sarah hugged me and said goodbye, then rode off. Ansel and I watched her drift away, getting smaller and smaller. Neither of us could figure out what to say, so Ansel took my hand. For a few seconds, I left my hand in his. The touch of his skin, no matter how brief or unexpected, brought sensations I had no name for. They weren't just physical. The physical stuff was no surprise. I'd learned long before that my body had a will of its own. Ansel's touch was different. It was as if some knowledge was being passed through the skin, an understanding that seeped through pores. Sometimes I thought he was the only person in the world who knew who I was.

But now he was only trying to be kind, feeling sorry for me. I pulled away.

"What's the matter?" he said.

"It just hasn't been a real good day."

"There's something else. What?"

I could see his feelings were hurt, and I was sorry for that. "Pay no attention to me, Ansel. I'm all mixed up. I've got to go."

"I'll ride with you," he said.

"Aren't you supposed to be with Susan?"

"You're my friend. I'm supposed to be with you."

We got on the bikes and headed toward the moon. And in the darkness and the distance that separated my bike from his, Ansel couldn't see that I was crying. Pedaling hard, I fought the awful feeling—not at all new—of how painful it is to hide things and to know that the people you love are doing the same.

six

I didn't notice my mother standing near the bleachers until there were only ten minutes left in the game, but she must have seen me block the other team's last try for a goal, the one that would have tied the game. Everybody was going crazy, lifting me up. We almost got a yellow flag for delay of game.

I thought I'd be thrilled to have her see that play. But I wasn't sure I cared anymore. When the game ended and everything calmed down, I walked over to her. She was smiling. Success always got my mother's attention.

"Congratulations," she said.

"Thanks."

"It was close."

"That's okay. It landed our way," I said. "I thought you left for Chicago this morning."

"I did some prep work at the office. I booked a flight for this evening."

"Why?"

"Because I wanted to see your game." She said it as if I'd asked a silly question.

I wondered how much of it she had actually seen. "What brought that on?"

"Morgan, the Chicago trip has been scheduled for weeks. I can't always change these things." I turned, looked back toward the field. What if Grandpa hadn't died when he did? Would she have taken off for Chicago while he was on his deathbed? "And I thought maybe you'd want to talk." She put her hand to my hair, tucked a loose strand behind my ear. The gesture felt so familiar, yet I didn't know what to make of it. She was like a performer, someone who studies her lines.

"I tried that already, remember?"

Mom let out a breath, annoyed I guess. I didn't care. The wind began to pick up, teasing the leaves on the great oaks that lined the long lane to the parking area. "There's not a whole lot more I can say about him," she said. I wasn't sure I'd heard her right. "Your father said he talked to you."

"And that's supposed to cover it?"

"Morgan—"

"He was my grandfather. How can there be no more you can say?"

"Grandpa was your grandfather," she corrected me sharply. Then she took a breath. "Oh, Morgan," she said, her tone different, as if annoyed at herself. "Sooner or later you'll come to your own conclusions about all this. But try to understand that I was doing what I thought was best for all of us. It was my way of protecting you."

"Couldn't you have done that without lying?"

She seemed to be struggling with something she wanted to say. Her voice was unsteady. "All my father ever brought anybody was pain." She stopped again to get control. "Why would I want to share that with people I care about? I never told you lies."

"Never told lies?" I said, my voice rising. "How did I get the idea that Stephen Dubrowski was my grandfather?"

The girls gathered near the bus were looking our way. My mother saw we were attracting attention and spoke in a harsh whisper. "He *was* your grandfather. He was married to your grandmother."

"Stop it. You know what I mean. You called him Dad." She had made me believe that was the whole story, as if Grandpa could make up for everything she'd hidden from me.

"That's right, but I never said he was my father."

"You knew what I thought. You never set me straight. What kind of truth is that?"

"A lot better than the real truth."

"Who gets to decide that? You?" The imperious way she made up her mind about what other people were entitled to know made me sick. I was like an underling.

"I had to make a judgment."

"You had no right. Terence Mulvaney didn't belong to just you."

"Belong?" The word made her laugh. "To belong to someone, you have to care about them. You have to make a connection. Believe me. My father never belonged to anyone."

"He belonged to Clover, didn't he?"

Mom shrugged her shoulders. "Maybe he changed as he got older. I have no idea."

"Or maybe she gave him half a chance." I realized how ridiculous I sounded, defending someone I would never even meet.

Mom adjusted the shoulder strap of her bag, stood straighter, as if we'd come to some line she wasn't going to cross. "Believe that if you want to," she said, her voice level. "But keep in mind that there are things you don't understand."

"Yeah, especially if you won't explain them to me," I said, because I could see she thought that settled things, as if none of it had anything to do with me. She wanted to short circuit this, but I wasn't letting her off that easy. "Why did your brother Michael go to Ireland to live?"

She took a step away, toward the parking lot. She looked tired. "I can't. Please don't ask me to do this anymore. I can't." She took out her car keys, glanced toward the bus. "Are you going with the team? Or do you want to ride with me?"

"I'll take the bus."

She leaned over to kiss my cheek. "Congratulations, Morgan. You were great," she said. "I'll see you when I get back." She headed to her car without looking back at me.

I watched her walk away, so tall and proud, regal. And I wondered about the shame she felt about her father. I'd felt it a little, too, when I saw the awful neighborhood he'd lived in, and especially when I told Ansel and Sarah about him. Still, I couldn't shake the feeling—crazy as it was—that something had been stolen from me. Bad or good, Terence Mulvaney was my grandfather, and that had been taken away. I wanted to know what he was like. Friends of the family had always remarked on how much like Grandpa I was, always curious about things, always ready to help. I was secretly glad they didn't think I was like my mother—strictly business, so intense. But what kind of a man was Terence Mulvaney? Was I like him at all? From the little Clover had told me, he sounded outgoing and pretty funny.

I reached into the side pocket of my gym bag, felt the edges of the little photo. Tucked beside it was my MetroCard for the subway. I thought of what Clover had said in her letter. "Brooklyn is not so far after all." I knew where I had to go to get my answers.

seven

I'd been awake for a long while, but it was still so dark out. The night didn't seem to want to give up its turn. A grim, gray sky made the air cold and damp. More rain was on the way, and the birds had nothing to say to each other. I got up, got dressed, then slipped back into bed, listening for my father to be up. I didn't want to tell him I was going to Brooklyn, so I didn't leave the house until after he did, and that was way past ten, but he was used to my slow starts on Saturdays.

The streets of Brooklyn were no less gray; the rain had erased the colors, dim as they were. Nothing welcomed me. But I knew this was where I needed to be. I wasn't nearly as frightened as I had been the first time. The squalor was not as shocking, and the old woman's building didn't seem so strange a destination. Inside, the smell in the halls took me by surprise. I had forgotten the smell.

I climbed the six flights, going over everything I wanted to ask her. She might not have all the answers, but whatever she knew would be a start. I couldn't stay long. It was already noon.

I knocked softly on 6B and waited. No one came to the door. I knocked again, harder, and soon footsteps were approaching. The door opened as far as the chain would allow, and I saw Clover peering out. "Ah, it's you," she said, as if I'd taken longer than necessary to go out for some groceries. She closed the door to take the chain off, then opened it wide and beckoned me in.

Clover took my damp rain slicker and hung it on the coat rack by the door. Wet from my walk from the subway in the misty rain, it hung limply in the corner, like a punished child. I thought about greeting her with a hug, but she seemed self-conscious, stiff, and the moment passed as she moved us quickly into the kitchen. Clover had just made tea, and I accepted a cup. Refusing it might have been some terrible Celtic insult.

I took the same chair I had taken the last time, watched her pour. "What brings you here, child?"

I shrugged. "I don't know."

She sat down across from me, unconvinced. "Suit yourself."

"I have some questions, I guess."

She nodded, as if she'd been expecting this.

"About Terence Mulvaney."

Clover let out a breath, as if her suspicions were confirmed. "Have you talked with your mother?"

"It's no use."

She sipped the tea. "And how old are you now?"

"Sixteen."

"Sure, you look older than that. But it's time enough still." She smoothed the tablecloth before her with a sweep of her arm, as if clearing the way for what was to come. "What is it you want to know?"

"I want to know everything," I told her, "about Terence Mulvaney, about Michael, about you, all of it."

Clover nodded, looked up to the ceiling, as if to remember where she'd put what I wanted. "All right then," she said, and began. She talked about coming to America as a young girl; meeting her husband, a Brooklyn policeman later killed in a car accident; her child, who died as a baby from meningitis. Before long, the tea was cold and she got up to put on a fresh pot.

I leaned on my elbows, my head in my hands, attentive, eager for her to come to the part when she met Mulvaney. The rain had stopped and the sun's glow filled the room like soft music.

Clover sat down again and in the light I could see the delicate white hairs on her chin. The glow softened her face, made her look vulnerable. "What was he like?" I said.

"What was he like? Do you mean your uncle Michael?" she said.

"No, Terence Mulvaney."

"Well, you're best to judge that for yourself," she said, and looked at the clock on the wall.

I was confused. "But I hardly have anything to go on," I told her. "My mother has nothing good to say about him. But there has to be more to it than that. I thought maybe you could tell me what he was like when you met him?"

Clover sighed. "He was incorrigible back then. But that was who he was. Always in trouble. I enjoyed him. That was the heart of it. I'd make him go to Mass when I could. He'd oblige me if he was looking to make amends—not to the Lord, of course, but to me," she said, and winked as if I were in on the joke. The memory in her smile lingered for a long while before she straightened up, turned toward me. "I didn't know what to make of you finally showing up on Tuesday to see your uncle's grave," she said. "I wondered if your mother knew you were coming."

"She didn't."

"I thought . . . but of course I was wrong."

"Thought what?"

"I thought it was time. That your mother was ready to be done with the past."

"I don't think so. She gets very uncomfortable when I ask her about any of it."

"I'm not saying she hasn't got a right," said Clover, "but your mother is stuck somewhere, in a time that's over now. Has been for years."

"Why does she have a right?"

"Your grandfather wasn't the best of fathers, but . . . "

"Clover, I know it seems to you like he was my grandfather ... but I had a grandfather ... Grandpa ... and I wish you wouldn't call anyone else that. It isn't right."

"Not right. I see," she said, but her look told me she didn't. "All I mean to say is he had his faults in those days but a good heart." She sounded defensive, as if seeing that the man was about to be rejected yet again by a new generation. "I know he's not what Hallmark has in mind in their Father's Day cards." I waited for more. It came reluctantly. "He drank. Couldn't hold a job. And he ... well, no man has a right to treat a woman that way."

"What way?"

Clover seemed unwilling to explain. "He was a different man when I met him, starting to feel things, realize what he'd lost." She folded her napkin over and over, nervous. She couldn't seem to settle back in her chair. "By then your mother had disowned him. Your grandmother had found a good man. Michael was gone to Ireland to escape the chaos, lived with his aunt. Terence would get a postcard from Pete now and then. That was it. He was alone," she said, her voice trailing to a whisper.

"Why couldn't they forgive him?"

"I think Pete and Michael did. At least they were willing to forget. But it's not my business to be talkin' to you about that."

I could see I'd reached a dead end. "Were you in love with him?" I whispered.

Clover smiled. "It's no easy job to love a man like Terence." She paused. "He didn't think he had a right. His life was cluttered with things like that, things he longed for but had no right to."

"Like my mother?"

She nodded. "There's a card he showed me once, a Valentine's card she made for him when she was eight or nine. It had a great big heart on the front with 'Daddy' written big as life." Clover motioned with her fingers, as if drawing the cover of the card. "And inside she wrote 'please be mine' in letters hardly large enough to see, like it was something she had to keep hidden, like she was afraid to wish for it."

"Is the card here? Do you still have it?"

"No, darlin'. He has it," she said, one bony finger pointing toward the hall we'd entered from.

"What do you mean?"

"He'd never part with it."

"But how could he . . . I don't understand."

"It's not so hard to understand. It's one of the few things he has of hers."

"What . . . what do you mean?"

"Well, aside from the photos Pete sends him now and then."

"This doesn't make sense," I said. Weren't we talking about a dead man?

"I suppose it doesn't. I mean it can't be easy for him. But he likes seeing what you all look like."

"Wait a minute," I whispered, already breathless. "I thought he was . . . I thought he was dead." I felt my skin go cold.

"Dead?" Clover sputtered a bit of tea. "Who told you he was dead? Is that what your mother said to you?"

"Well, no, I guess she didn't . . . she didn't say that exactly . . . but the way she talks makes it seem that way, and even you . . ."

"Why, we've been talking so long, he must be home by now." The old woman turned and checked the clock again. "Yes, I'm sure he's home by now."

"Home? What do you mean home?"

"His apartment. It's downstairs. He . . . Morgan, I don't know what your mother has told you or not told you, or how you ever wound up here, but . . ."

"You mean he's in this building? He lives here?"

"Yes. Of course. He's lived here nearly as long as I have," she said, getting up and heading toward the hall, excited now. "You'll be wantin' to meet him. I'll go and . . ."

"Clover, wait. I don't think . . . I . . . "

Clover turned, stood in the doorway. "He's your grandfather, Morgan," she said firmly, as if this time she'd tolerate no argument about it. "And I swore to him that if you came back, I'd let him know straight away."

There was nothing else to do. She walked out of the kitchen, into the hall. I heard her close the apartment door. I sat very still, my insides trembling, and stared at the window. From where I sat, I could see rooftops, and it seemed as if I'd fallen into a picture in some book, into a fantasy. I struggled with the feeling that what I was about to do was wrong. I couldn't shake the uneasiness, but the excitement was so much more powerful.

eight

Their voices reached me first. Clover's was deliberate, as if she were giving instructions; the other was deep, questioning. Then I heard the apartment door close and the sounds of their footsteps, light and heavy, coming along the hall toward the kitchen. I turned and saw Clover in the doorway, made small by the huge silhouette of the man behind her. I could see mostly his face and shoulders. He had wavy white hair that curled around his thick neck, and tired blue eyes that were already drinking me in. Clover stepped inside, and the big man followed. He took up so much space in the little room that he seemed to absorb everything, even the sunlight on his ruddy skin and snowy hair.

"Morgan, this is Terence Mulvaney," she said, her voice charged with the moment, as if it were something grand. I stood up, and the old man extended his hand in greeting. The sleeves of his sweater, too short for him, had cuffs stained with something gray. His wrists were freckled and covered with white hair. I'd never seen hands so large. I couldn't keep mine from trembling. His touch was shy, uncertain, but he held on to my hand a long while, and that calmed me somehow.

"Sit down. Sit down, both of ya," said Clover, eager to get on with things. We did as we were told. The room stayed quiet for what seemed like a long time. I had to avert my eyes from the old man's constant stare.

"So," he said finally. That's all. Just the one syllable. It wasn't a question. It was more like a kind of introduction, but to what

I had no idea. I let a moment pass. "So," he said again. His voice was large, the brogue thicker than Clover's. "It's Morgan they named you, is it?"

"Morgan, yes," I said.

"Morgan," he repeated, his disapproval evident. "Sounds like the name of someone puttin' on airs. Is it from your father's side then?"

"No. I don't think so."

"What does it mean?"

"Mean? I don't know."

"A name has a meaning, child. It's chosen for a reason. It's not supposed to come out of a hat."

"I don't know what it means." I felt as if I was being scolded for something I'd had no part in. "I guess they just liked it."

"And how do *you* like it?"

It was strange that he should ask this, because I'd always secretly disliked my name. "It's okay," I shrugged. "I mean I'm not crazy about it, but I'm used to it."

"We'll have to think of something else then," he said matter-of-factly. "Won't we, Clover?"

I knew it was a presumptuous thing for him to say, but I liked it. It felt as if he was staking a claim to something. They got quiet, and I wondered if they would decide on a name right then and there. He seemed to be studying my face, or trying to remember it, as if he'd seen me before but wasn't sure where.

"I . . . I know who you are," I whispered finally. "I know you're my grandfather. Clover told me."

For the first time, he looked away from me, then spoke as if braced for an attack. "And what do you make of that news?"

"I don't understand why it had to be a secret."

"I'm hardly a fond memory."

"Can I ask you something?" I said.

"I don't suppose there's any way of stopping you." He took a pack of Camels from his shirt and lit one. Clover began to object, but he waved her off.

"Why didn't you stay her father?" I said. "I mean why didn't you stay in touch with her? Maybe that's why she's so mad, because you stayed away."

"I stayed where I belonged. Let's leave it at that."

"But didn't you care about her?"

He looked tired. "That's why I let her be," he said.

"But didn't you . . ."

Clover stood up, uncomfortable with my questions. Maybe she was afraid they'd make him feel bad. "Tell your grandfather what you're studying in school," she said.

Your grandfather. It sounded so strange, so wrong. "The usual stuff," I answered half-heartedly. "History, math. My friends and I are writing a paper now. We have to research and write a report."

"A report about what?" Clover said.

"About homeless people in America."

"I guess you didn't have to think hard to come up with that one," she said. "You can't walk down the street without stepping over the poor souls."

I didn't know what to say to this. There were no homeless people in the street in Princeton, although I knew what she meant. I'd seen some on the walk from the subway and even more in Penn Station. "We need to trace the history of it," I told her, "find out how it got this bad."

Clover looked confused. "Your books and research will tell you that, will they?"

"There are quite a few books about it. We found one about welfare reform after World War II."

"Ah," she said.

"And one on the Great Society in the sixties."

"You don't say?"

"I'm sure the books will tell you quite a bit," said Mr. Mulvaney. "But none of 'em is going to answer your question." I looked at him, confused. "If you want to know how it got so bad that someone is sleeping in a refrigerator box, you've got to ask him yourself."

"Ask who?"

"The man in the box."

"But it isn't just one person's story we're after," I said. "We need a wider perspective, an historical . . . "

"Then talk to his neighbor on the park bench and the one across the street in the doorway," he said almost harshly.

"But, you see, this isn't just a problem in Brooklyn," I said. "It's all across the country. We're supposed to get at the underlying reasons for it."

"Oh, I do see. I see it all the time. So you want to know why these people have nowhere to go?"

"Well, yes."

"That's a different question altogether," he said. "That's something we need to ask each other."

The look in his eye made it hard to look back at him. I felt bad. I wondered what kind of person I seemed like to him. He and Clover clearly didn't have much money, probably never did, but I didn't want him to think I was spoiled or that I couldn't see how terrible it must be for people in such situations. Except I couldn't imagine what it would feel like to have nowhere to live.

"Well, I'm sure you'll do a fine job of it," said Clover. "You can see what a bright girl she is, Terence."

"Your mother was a brilliant student. Brilliant," said Mr. Mulvaney. "Pete was another story altogether. He didn't come around 'til college. Then he caught up just fine." I wanted this, to hear him talk of my mother as a girl. "She was like a racehorse, that one. Always wanting to come in first. Nothing else was good enough. Not for M&M."

"Where did you live when she was little?"

"We lived in the Bronx." He glanced at Clover, puzzled.

"She knows nothing," she told him. "Not a thing."

"Is that where my mother was born?" I asked.

"Yes, she was born there."

"Do you have any other pictures of her? I mean from when she was young?"

"I do. Yes."

"I showed her the one you did of Michael," Clover laughed. "He got points for being handsome."

"You mean the drawing in the other room?" I said. "You did that?"

"Of course he did. Didn't I tell you that?"

"No. I don't think so. It's really good. You're very talented."

"Thank you," said Mr. Mulvaney, looking sheepish about it.

"And you have drawings of my mother when she was younger?"

"A few."

"But when—"

"I did them from photos," he said, seeing my confusion. "Your uncle Pete would give them to me."

"I'd love to have one."

He nodded.

"And Michael? Do you have more of Michael?"

"I do," he said, his voice dropping.

"I'd really like to see them. And to hear more about him," I said, not sure if it would be too hard for him to talk about his son.

Mr. Mulvaney glanced at Clover, hesitant, then sighed. "Michael was no stranger to trouble. When he left home, he lived with my sister in Derry, in the very house I grew up in, 'til he got married. His boys are there still."

"And his wife?"

"Killed," said Clover.

"Sniper. Probably meant for him."

"She wasn't twenty-five yet," said Clover.

"Did he go to Ireland to join the IRA?" They didn't ask me how I knew he'd been in it, so I didn't say.

"No," said Mr. Mulvaney. "Michael didn't want any part of fightin'. He joined up with the Civil Rights Movement. Nonviolence, you see. There was a huge march that year, 1978."

"Ten thousand people," said Clover.

Mr. Mulvaney nodded. "All of 'em walking the same route the protestors walked ten years before."

"Four miles they walked," said Clover. "All the way from Coalisland to Dungannon."

"A peaceful protest," Mr. Mulvaney insisted, even as he brought his fist down on the table with a thud.

"But it was IRA nonetheless, Terence," said Clover.

"There's no denyin' it," Mr. Mulvaney conceded. "Before the year was out, they were calling him Father Michael."

"You mean for the nonviolence?" I said.

"No, for the cassock he wore to run guns through Belfast."

"It's a miracle he lived as long as he did," said Clover.

"Couldn't you stop him? I mean from getting involved in that kind of thing," I said. "My mother calls them criminals."

"How do you tell a young, headstrong fella to stand by while innocent men are being killed and tortured in prison?" he said, his voice getting louder. "Or when they can't get work to support their families because they made the mistake of being born Catholic? He wouldn't have listened to me."

I wondered what I would have done if things like that were happening to people I cared about.

"He never did any harm himself," said Clover. "Never." I caught the look Mr. Mulvaney gave her, as if she were splitting hairs.

"How did he die?"

"Lung cancer," she said. "He was sick for a long while," said Clover.

"Is that why he came back to the United States?"

"No, he came back ten years ago," she said.

"He was in trouble with that new faction of the IRA," said Mr. Mulvaney.

"New faction?"

"They were against the peace talks, against any terms with the British."

"And for good reason," said Clover.

"Ah, woman, don't start. Anyway, Michael felt it was better for him to leave. He wasn't much help to them anymore, after his wife was killed."

"What about you? Were you involved, too?"

"That's all in the past now." I could see he wanted to leave it at that.

"But you were?"

"I got out of the way of things. I had no stomach for it. Blasting the Black and Tans off our front steps the way my father did was one thing. This was quite another."

"That's enough of your talking," Clover said to Mr. Mulvaney. "This girl has to get home."

That was true, though I could see she was coming to his rescue because I wanted to hear more. But the light in the room was getting thin. It must have been almost three o'clock, and I couldn't stay much longer. "Yes, I do," I said.

"How are you getting there?" he said.

"I take the subway to Penn Station."

"Not by yourself?"

"I'll be fine."

"You'll not be travelin' by yourself in this city. I'll go with you." He saw the look on my face and held up his hand as if to reassure me. "Just as far as Penn Station. You can go off on your own from there."

"You really don't have to," I told him, but I was glad. I wanted to do this ordinary thing with him, maybe pretend that it was something we'd been doing together for years.

We got our coats on and Clover gave me a stiff hug. Outside, the sun was very low, the streets getting dark. I was glad not to be alone. With the old man at my side, I drew glances from the young men but none of the comments I had before.

"Do you know which train to get?" he asked me, slowing his pace. I was having trouble keeping up with him.

"It's the D."

"The D. Of course. I don't get to the city much. I forget these things. That's the bad part about getting old. The forgetting. Of course, the stuff you wouldn't mind forgetting holds on like a monkey."

I asked him if he still worked and he told me about his job at the warehouse just a few blocks away. "They just need a good mule is all," he said. "They have me lifting all day long, and they even want me there on weekends sometimes. But they let me go home early most days. So that's good."

After a block or so, he had something he wanted to ask me about. He started, then stopped, then tried again. I figured it was about my mother. It was. "Would you mind my askin' how she is?" he finally said.

"She's fine," I told him. "She travels a lot. She's a consultant. Her clients are all over the place."

"Yes, yes," he said, as if he knew these things already, probably from Uncle Peter. "I guess what I mean to say is what is she like?"

I didn't know what to tell him. "She's busy," I said, "always busy."

"She's important. That's clear," he said, his chin up just a bit, his chest seeming to swell. But I could see he wanted something more.

"She's a little superstitious," I offered, wondering if this was the kind of thing he was looking for. "She won't let me open an umbrella indoors." He laughed at that. "She likes to sing, but only when she thinks no one can hear her. She loves old movies, even goofy ones with Fred Astaire." He waited for more, but I hesitated, not sure how much it was okay to tell this man about a daughter who'd crossed him out of her life. "And she writes poetry. She doesn't know I know that. Some of it is sad." He didn't say anything, but I heard a kind of sigh.

"Listen," he said. "You were askin' before why I stayed away."

"Yeah. I think maybe that's why she's been so angry."

"It's not something a girl like you could understand. You're a good girl. But people aren't always good. They do hurtful things. They try to stop, but they can't."

He thought I couldn't understand that, but I did. He looked at me as if I was some kind of got-bucks kid who'd never had trouble in her life, never had a disappointment. "That's not true," I told him, remembering the things I'd done in Chicago. "I *can* understand that."

"Well, I hope you never have to, because it was better for me not to be around your mother. The things I did made her very sad. They made everyone sad."

He was talking to me as if I were a child. "I've done bad things," I said, "things I wish I could have stopped."

He looked down at me, doubtful, amused really.

The entrance to the subway was just across the street, but the rain puddle by the curb was huge. We would have had to walk halfway down the side street to clear it. We hesitated, staring at the subway entrance just out of reach. I was about to suggest we head down the side street when he said, "Here. Let me." Before I could understand what he meant, I felt myself being lifted off the ground. He cleared the puddle in a few broad strides, with me in his arms. It was so silly, and so good.

I felt his scratchy chin against my forehead, took in his smell of soap and wool, a working man's smell. When he reached the sidewalk, he put me down with such care, like I was breakable, and I smiled at him.

"I see your mother when you smile like that," he said.

I could see this was hard for him, that it must have hurt to be reminded of her. I thanked him for taking me over the puddle, and we headed down the stairs into the subway. The train came quickly and he was silent for the entire ride. The car was crowded and we shared a metal pole to keep our balance. He stared over my head at the posters in Spanish above the windows, as if their messages required careful study. I stared mostly at his hand on the pole, the white hairs on his fingers, the rough skin, the cracked, wide fingernails. I raised my eyes to his face now and then but caught him looking down at me only once.

When the crackling voice announced 34th Street, I heard him say what sounded like, "Here we are then" as he put his hand on my elbow. We followed the crowd into the station and up the stairs into the cavernous place where passengers wait for their trains to be announced. He stopped, as if we'd reached some territory that was off limits. "You'll be fine from here then."

"Oh, yes," I told him, "fine."

"Good," he said, but still he stood, as if unable to leave me, maybe not sure how. A hug? A handshake? I saw he was at a loss.

The words came out before I'd given myself permission to say them, although they'd been in my head more than once on the subway. "I'm glad we met. I'd like to see you again."

That seemed to shake him free. He knew what to do now. But he avoided my eyes and looked down, shook his head. "We can't be doin' that." He stood up straighter. "Go on now," he said, motioning to the crowds behind me, "before you miss your train."

"Why not?" I said.

"You don't want to be talkin' to the likes of me."

"That's not true," I insisted and the rest came out before I could censor it. "You're my . . . my grandfather."

"Well, that was the Lord's plan, I suppose, starting out." We stood there, awkward, such an odd match, but no one noticed. A train was called and travelers hurried by. "There's one thing you might as well get straight in your head, child," he said. "Life doesn't always happen the way it's supposed to. There may be a grand plan, but more often than not somebody mucks it up."

"Can't we just talk sometimes?" My throat was tight. I didn't want to cry.

Mr. Mulvaney answered me carefully, the way you might break bad news to a child, someone who couldn't be expected to understand the real reasons for things. "I was reckless with my life, Morgan. There were good things in it. Beautiful things. And I didn't take care."

"I don't understand," I said.

He touched my fingertips so lightly that I might have missed it if I hadn't watched him do it. "I couldn't see what I was doing to people, and I lost them. There are mistakes you can't undo."

"What mistakes? What happened?"

He looked down at his shoes, and I could hear his breathing. He spoke softly. "And if you knew what happened, do you think you'd know me better, the person here with you now?"

"The past doesn't matter to me. I'm just trying to understand."

"I can't be doin' this," he said.

"Talking to me, you mean?" I said. He didn't answer me, but I didn't want to give up. I reached into my bag for my pen, but I had no paper, so I dug a napkin out of my pocket and wrote my number on it. "You can call me," I said, offering him the napkin. The limp paper hung there for a moment before he finally took it, without a word.

I didn't say goodbye. I turned away and headed for the waiting area. In a few steps, I turned around to look at him, but he was gone. Still, all the while, in the long moments before the train was called, I felt as if I was being watched.

nine

I recognized the whir of Ansel's bike, heard the gate close. His footsteps were noisy in the leaves. He found me at the base of the wall, near Mrs. R. Nelson Peabody. My legs were folded up in my arms, my head resting on my knees. I didn't look up.

"Morgan." He whispered my name, as if hesitating to wake a late sleeper. I looked up, and he could tell that I'd been crying. "Morgan," he said again, and settled next to me on the ground. "I got your text. What happened? Why weren't you at Sarah's?" We were supposed to meet at Sarah's this morning, then go to the library.

"She didn't call my house, did she?" I said, my voice husky from tears.

"No. With everything that's been going on—"

"Good."

"But where were you?"

"Brooklyn." He waited for more, but I didn't offer it.

"Maybe you shouldn't go there anymore. I mean if it makes you upset."

"He's not dead," I whispered, but my voice cracked and he couldn't make out what I'd said.

"What? What are you saying?" He turned my face toward his.

"Terence Mulvaney. My mom's father. He's alive."

"Holy—Did Clover tell you that?"

"Yes."

"Jeez, Morgan. That's incredible. Your mom—"

"I talked to him."

"You met him? You spoke with him?"

"Yes. He lives in Clover's building. She thought I knew he was alive. She didn't know my mother had . . . had kept that a secret, too." My voice began to break again, and this time Ansel put his arms around me.

"Oh, Morgan."

I buried my face in his shoulder. My breathing came in short little gasps, and I knew Ansel probably thought I was crying, but it wasn't tears making me breathless. It was Ansel. I closed my eyes, and he held me for what seemed like a long time. I surrendered to the movement of his breathing, until the world felt like it could be predictable again, normal—at least this little part of it. He pulled us down to the grass, his back against the wall, pulled me close to him. I felt the tension in his arms and wondered if he was nervous, too.

"What's he like?"

I laughed. "He's big and a little gruff, but he seems—I don't know—kind." I lifted my head from his shoulder and our noses touched. "He's really . . . he's big," I said, but I was having trouble putting thoughts together. "He must be six foot four," I whispered, and now there was no way to avoid Ansel's eyes. His look made me feel awkward and strange, so I lowered my gaze. Then something brushed my lips—something so soft—and I realized that it was Ansel's lips I was feeling and that he was going to kiss me. I thought of pushing him away, but he held me tighter, as if he knew what I was thinking. I gave in then, let him kiss me, remembering how often I'd imagined this. I put my arm around him. Almost immediately, he started to ease away. He was ending it already. I didn't want him to. I wanted to hold him tight, kiss him back just the way he'd kissed me, the way he seemed to want me to.

"Morgan, I'm sorry. I'm so sorry," he said, and sat up. "Please don't be mad at me."

"Mad? I . . . " but I caught the conflicted look on his face. Clearly this wasn't what he wanted.

"You're not mad at me, are you?" he said.

I scrambled to my feet. "No, of course not," I said, brushing the leaves from the back of my pants. "It's no big deal." His face changed at this, saddened, but I headed toward the bikes.

He caught up, a little breathless. "Tell me about Mulvaney."

"There's nothing to tell. It's no big deal."

"But you like him. You said he was nice."

"I like him," I said, and stood the bike up.

"Morgan, listen," Ansel said. There was concern in his voice, and he put his hand on my arm. "I don't want you to get the wrong idea about . . . "

I pulled away from him and got on my bike. "I won't," I told him. I'd made a fool of myself, but I wasn't stupid. He said something more, but by then I was too far away to hear him.

My phone began ringing as I entered the house. From the kitchen, I heard Louisa call my name, asking if I wanted dinner. I was afraid the call was Ansel, and I didn't want to take it. But it wasn't Ansel at all. The voice in the receiver seemed too large for it, too loud. I had to hold it away from my ear. It was Terence Mulvaney. "Yes," I answered. "This is Morgan."

"I was just wondering is all," he said, as if he were picking up again on a point he'd been making just moments ago. He must have been using a public phone, a place exposed to the traffic and wind. I waited for him to continue.

"You were saying you'd like to see some of the drawings."

"Yes."

"Well, the warehouse owner—he's a contractor—lets me keep some of them there. I thought maybe you'd like to come and have a look."

I was surprised. Earlier he'd been pretty clear that he didn't think it was a good idea to see me, but I wasn't about to derail this by asking why he'd changed his mind.

"Anyway, if you're interested—"

"Oh, I am."

"All right then," he said with surprise, as if he wasn't entirely sure my agreement was a good thing. "When can you come?"

"Well, I don't know."

"Are you free tomorrow?"

"Well—"

"Good. Let's make it three o'clock. You'll be long out of Mass by then."

I decided not to mention the last time I'd been to Mass.

"There's a large bookstore, one of the chains, a few blocks north of your subway station," he said. "Inside they've got a coffee shop. Find a table and wait there. I'll find you."

"Okay," I said, still wondering what had made him change his mind. Long after I hung up, I tried to pinpoint what it was about his voice that made him sound as if he were being forced into something he'd never intended.

ten

The bookstore was easy to find. I chose a table where I could watch the people enter from the street. Some came in as if on an urgent mission. They needed books the way they needed milk or bread. Others seemed noncommittal, as if something in the window had merely caught their eye. They wanted excitement maybe, or adventure, although they seemed unconvinced that they'd find it.

I spotted him across the street. He walked with the crowd at first, like a great mast above a deck of unruly sailors. Then, impatient with their pace, he broke away, crossing in the middle of the street. When he got closer to the window, he looked in, but my table was too far back for him to see me. He looked worried, uneasy. I wondered again what had made him change his mind about getting together, but before I could think much more about it, he was in the store and heading toward me.

The old man extended his hand. I shook it, but it was like trying to grasp a baseball mitt. "I was afraid you wouldn't wait," he said. "They were running late today. Sunday pays double time."

"I haven't been here very long."

"Good. Good," he said, but didn't sit down. He looked around, taking in the size of the place. "Quite a shop. It's bigger than the warehouse."

"Yes. It feels like a warehouse, too. I like the small bookstores better."

"But they don't have hot chocolate," he said with a grin. "Would you like some?"

"Sure, if you don't have to get back."

"I'm mostly done for the day."

"Hot chocolate sounds great then."

He headed for the counter, again dwarfing everyone around him. He was wearing a loose-fitting fatigue jacket, heavy construction boots, and paint-spotted pants frayed at the heel. His ruddy complexion and unruly white hair made him look like some scout from a band of conquering Celts, sent ahead to size up the town they were about to pillage.

When his turn came at the counter, I noticed he paid the cashier mostly with coins. The steaming cups were all but lost in his broad hands as he brought them to the table and settled into the chair across from me. This took a bit of doing, since the space was small for him. He cleared his throat and jerked his head in a self-conscious way but said nothing and didn't quite look at me.

I still wasn't convinced that he wanted to be there. He sipped his coffee and watched the passersby through the window. At one point he reached into his jacket for his cigarettes, then remembered aloud that smoking was not allowed. I left the silence alone for a little longer before I said anything. "Are you sure this is what you want? Seeing me, I mean?"

"I'm just not very good at this," he said. His eyes softened, his jaw slowly gave up some resolve. "I can hardly believe you're here, right across from me like this."

I smiled. "Neither can I." I couldn't help laughing. "I mean until I met Clover on Tuesday I didn't even know you existed."

He smiled into his cup. "Well, we're making progress then, aren't we?"

"Yes," I said, but another awkward silence followed.

He moved his body to face me, purposefully, ready to begin some task. "I'm hoping to get to know you better." I nodded. "Tell me about your dad. What's he like?" he said off-handedly. Still, I wondered what he was really after.

"Oh," I shrugged, "he's, you know, he's a great guy, really smart."

"I've heard that from your uncle Pete."

"He teaches physics. He's kind of quiet, I guess. But not really, not when he's interested in something."

"Namely you, I'm sure."

My mind went blank for a second. Only a feeling registered, a longing. A time just a few years ago came back, when my dad had been a much bigger part of my life, when he hadn't been so preoccupied, so absent. "I don't see him that much, really."

Mr. Mulvaney looked at me more closely, as if I'd given something away. "Does he keep you on a short leash, is that it?" he laughed. "With charms like yours, I can see why he would."

I smiled at the compliment. "He's pretty reasonable actually. He likes to know where I am. They both do, of course." But even as I spoke the words, I remembered the night just weeks before when I'd called from Ansel's at ten o'clock to say I'd be late, only to find that neither of my parents was home yet. And they weren't together.

"Reasonable. Good," Mr. Mulvaney said, as if this were important to him personally and not just an observation. "Easygoing then, you'd say?"

"Oh, yes. Definitely. He never gets upset about small stuff."

"Good. Good," he said, nodding his head. "So tell me how you spend your time. Who are your friends? What kind of mischief do you get yourselves into?" he winked. He seemed less like a man on a mission and more like an old friend now. He pumped me with questions about the most mundane things, probed for the smallest details. He asked me what I remembered about Chicago, about California. He even asked me about Grandpa, and I was sure that was hard for him, hearing about the person who had taken his place.

"And your mother," he said, lowering his voice, as if he shouldn't be heard mentioning her. "What did she say when you told her?"

"Told her?"

"That you met me?"

"She doesn't know yet," I said. I, too, had lowered my voice almost to a whisper. "She's in Chicago. She won't be back until the end of the week. I'll tell her then, I guess."

"The end of the week. I see," he said, as if making a mental note of this. He got quiet again until finally he sighed. "She's not likely to welcome the news."

"I guess not."

"There's nothing I can do about that." He shook his head, and I wondered if some old phantom had come to haunt him again, one he'd grown tired of shooing away and made a truce with instead. He moved his cup aside. "Well then, do you want to see some drawings?"

"Absolutely."

We headed toward the door and when we got outside, he looked at me and smiled, his face relaxing for the first time. "You look so much like her." I didn't know what to say.

He said the warehouse was about five blocks away, but the building appeared a block sooner than I expected. I spotted the sign: Superior Acoustics. It was a small, single-story building painted in a color that appeared pink in that light. It had no windows, except for a small, square space in the narrow door beneath the sign. I got on my toes to look through it, but the glass was dirty and I could hardly see inside. Mr. Mulvaney got out a ring of keys and opened the door. Materials were layered high along all the walls, and stacks of boxes of various shapes and heights rose from the floor here and there in no particular order.

"Wow, it's really big."

"It is."

I kept my jacket on because it wasn't very warm in the place. "Chilly," I said.

"A little work would warm you up," he said, looking to see if I was game.

"Sure. What can I do?"

He walked me toward some boxes that had been torn open and cast aside. "These are ceiling tiles," he said. "The buggers can't be bothered to read the labels on the boxes, so they tear them open to see the style. And sometimes they take just the few that they need." I wasn't sure why I needed to know all this, but I listened. "Sort through these open boxes and try to fill in what's missing. Each box should have twenty-four tiles in it."

"Oh, I get it."

"Good," he said, and started checking some things that had been delivered that morning. He asked me questions while we worked and listened to me talk about Ansel and Sarah, about school. After a little while, he went into a back room for a moment and came out with two sodas. "Well, I think that will do," he said.

"So do I get to see your drawings?"

"I almost forgot. They're nothing much, you know."

"I'd really like to see them."

"All right then," he said, and walked to a far corner of the warehouse, a catch-all place of boxes and brooms and shelving. He pulled a wide, flat box from one of the shelves and removed the lid, searched inside a bit as if trying to decide which to pull out. He came back with four drawings, each about twelve by fourteen. The one on top, the one he showed me first, was a landscape of mountains with a lake and a tiny little house at the shoreline. "That's Strathfoyle, just outside of Derry, where my grandmother was born. Right in that house."

"It's beautiful," I said. It really was. It was done in pencil, only grays, no color, but there was something so warm about it. You could see he must have loved the place.

The next two were of Michael, but he was younger than in the one in Clover's living room. He was maybe twenty, laughing. In the other he was with a girl, very pretty. "Was that his wife?"

"Yes. Kate," he said.

"She was lovely." Everything about these drawings was lovely, haunting almost. They made me a little breathless. He was really talented.

"And here's one for you," he said. It was my mother. I knew it immediately, though the girl in the drawing was no more than fourteen or so. She was looking up from opening a present, delighted with it.

"You did this from a photo?" I was afraid I'd cry, not just because of how carefully the work had been done, but because of the longing in it. It was on his face now.

"Yes."

I held it up higher, so it would catch more of the ceiling light. I examined it, fascinated. She did look like me. And I recognized something else, something in her eyes that was like me, too, something searching.

"I was wondering," he said. I waited for him to go on, but he was having trouble.

"What?"

"Do you think she'd see me? Your mother, I mean." He was busy rolling up the drawing and placing it into a tube, trying to make the question seem casual. I stared at him. The idea seemed so foolish, almost absurd. It was the last thing she'd want, but I didn't say so. He searched my face for a clue. "I know she's been pretty angry, but after what's happened, you and me I mean, maybe she might take a different view."

"I just don't know," I said, even though I did.

"Would it be askin' too much for you to broach the subject with her? See what kind of response you get?"

"I can do that. Sure," I said, although I dreaded it. I didn't even know how I was going to tell her I'd met him.

He patted my shoulder. "Good girl."

"May I ask you something?" He didn't say yes, but I asked anyway. "Why didn't you ever try to see me?"

"It's not important now. That's your mother's business to be tellin' you anyway. Not mine."

"She won't talk about it," I said, angry. "How am I supposed to understand any of it?"

He seemed taken aback by my boldness. "And what makes you think our telling you would mean you'd understand? There isn't a lot of sense to it. It was my doing, not your mother's. Understand that much anyway."

"But what about me? Something was taken away from me."

"I'm no great loss, child, not to anyone."

"Clover likes you."

"Yes," he said with kind of a laugh. "Mostly."

"And Clover has memories of you, even things that belong to you, things you gave her. I don't have anything like that."

"Your mother gave you something better."

"No, she didn't. She kept everything from me."

"Stop that now. She gave you a real grandfather, somebody you can look back on and be glad about." I thought of Grandpa and how I missed him, but remembering Grandpa didn't make it better. I still felt cheated.

"I'll always love Grandpa. That's not the question, and you know it." He lowered his eyes. "You were supposed to be my grandfather. If that mattered to you, you'd have come to see me."

"You were an infant."

"I haven't been an infant in a long while." I was surprised at how angry I felt—and at how badly I didn't want to be angry at him. "So what do we do about it now?"

He touched my hand to calm me. "We do what we came to do. Get to know each other. And when you do, maybe you'll make up your own mind about me."

He must have known I was willing to do that. Still, when I nodded he seemed uncertain about it, as if he was giving in to a temptation he never thought he'd face.

I realized the daylight was gone. There were so few windows in the place that it was hardly noticeable. I looked at my watch. "I'd better get back," I told him.

"Yes, it's quittin' time," he said. We headed for the door and he shut off some lights. Outside it was windy, and he took my elbow and guided me back to the subway. I told him he didn't need to go with me the whole way, but he insisted. At Penn Station, he kept his hand on my arm, a light touch that made no claims and gave no direction. I saw the glances he drew as we moved past the shops toward the heart of the station, where the big board would display my train's track. When we got there, the train had already pulled in.

Mr. Mulvaney cleared his throat, struggled with something he wanted to say. "I want you to know," he started, but the rest didn't come. I looked at him. He glanced at the clock above the board, as if defeated by circumstances he couldn't control. "I just . . . I . . . "

"It's okay," I told him. "It's okay."

"Yes," he whispered. "Everything will be okay."

"I like you very much," I said, but immediately wished I hadn't. It sounded so much like a judgment.

He smiled at that. "Now, you know what Clover would say to that, don't you?"

"No, what?"

"Give it time."

I laughed, and the last call came for my train. "When do I get to hear about you?"

"Me?" he said, waving his hand, as if there was nothing worth talking about.

"Yeah, I want to know all about you."

"Then come again. Come anytime. Come to Clover's place."

"Maybe I will."

"Well, so long then," he said. I nodded and held the sleeve of his jacket, got on my toes, kissed his cheek quickly, and ran toward the platform for my train.

eleven

Ansel tried to talk to me in the morning and again in second period, but I managed to keep things from getting past how are you. He didn't know I'd gone to see Mr. Mulvaney the day before. I wanted to tell him about it, but I couldn't. Every time I looked at him, I'd replay what happened in the cemetery a million times over, think about how good it had felt when he was holding me—until he'd remembered it was me he was kissing and couldn't apologize fast enough.

The last period of the day was about to end, and I was in a kind of bubble. I didn't want to let anyone in and I didn't really want to get out. I liked it there, where I could think about Clover and Mr. Mulvaney, forget about figuring out my parents—and now Ansel had been added to the list of mysteries.

The bell startled me and I dropped my book, but I was still one of the first out the door. It was cool outside. I wished I'd worn something warmer. Near the corner, a friend of mine called me, but I pretended I didn't hear her. I just wanted to find Sarah and bring her to my house so I could show her the drawing, but there was no sign of her, so I headed for her house. After a block or two, I felt somebody tugging at my bookbag.

"Where's the fire?" Ansel said. He had a look on his face that I couldn't read, like he was embarrassed and worried and happy all at the same time.

"Ansel."

"Yeah. Remember me? What's going on?" As if he didn't know. He hadn't called my cell or my house since Saturday, when I'd seen him at the cemetery, and I didn't need anyone to explain what that meant.

"Nothing," I told him.

"I have to go to Mr. Kinsey's. Want to walk me?"

"I've got to get to Sarah's."

He glanced at me, waited a beat. "Are you sure there's nothing wrong?"

"Nothing." Nothing I was ready to tell him about.

I waited for him to head back toward town, but he just kept walking beside me. "I thought you had to get to the store," I said.

"I'll get there. I'll walk you home first."

Oh, God. I wanted him to just leave me alone.

"So what were you up to yesterday? I thought I'd see you after the game."

I wished I could tell him I'd had an appointment with my long-lost grandpa, but I didn't want to get into a discussion. I wanted him gone. "I had stuff to do," I told him.

He dropped back, got behind me, and pulled at my bookbag so I couldn't keep going. "Ansel, stop," I said. "Let go."

He tugged at me until he got us close to a tree, then dropped his bookbag down and took mine off my shoulder. "I've got a pebble in my sneaker," he said, and sat down on the ground among the leaves and took off his sneaker.

We were quiet for a little bit. "Want to go for a ride?"

He meant in his father's car. We did that sometimes now that he had his driving permit. "I can't."

"Why not?"

"You have to go to Mr. Kinsey's."

"That's why *I* can't. What's your excuse?"

"Just things to do."

"You're not mad about what happened Saturday, are you?"

"Nothing happened Saturday." He got quiet, and I felt bad. Talk about twisted. Why should I feel bad when he was the one being a jerk? "I went to see Mr. Mulvaney yesterday."

"You went to Brooklyn?"

"Yeah. To the warehouse where he works."

"What was that like?"

"It was kind of nice. I don't mean the place. I mean just hanging out with him."

"Yeah?"

"Really nice, actually. He's old-fashioned, but it makes him interesting. Wants to know everything about me, asked me a million questions." I stopped, because I realized how I sounded, like Mr. Mulvaney was important to me or something.

"That's great," Ansel said. He seemed happy for me. "You going to visit him again?"

"Yes, I like him. And he's really talented. You should see the drawings he does. That's why I want to talk to Sarah. I think her mom might want to see this stuff."

"You mean sell it?" He sounded like he was having trouble believing Mr. Mulvaney could have any talent.

"Why not? He's really good. He gave me a drawing he did of my mom when she was young. He drew it from a photograph."

"Morgan, real artists use models. They don't—"

"What do you know about real artists?"

"Well, I know none of the artists Sarah's mom works with does that."

I didn't say anything, but it bothered me that he was ready to assume Mr. Mulvaney's work was no good. Just because he was an old guy living in a rat hole of a building in Brooklyn, Ansel figured he couldn't be an artist, at least not the kind that Sarah's mother would represent. He had a point. A lot of her "people," as she called them, were graduates of fancy art schools. They lived in converted barns near New Hope and

Yardley and called it rustic because deer showed up in the front yard now and then.

"When are you going back to Brooklyn again?" he said.

"Tomorrow. Today I'm going to talk to Sarah."

"Not about the old guy's drawings?" He obviously thought there was no chance she'd like Mr. Mulvaney's work.

"Yes."

"What happened with him anyway? You really hit it off?"

"I told you. He's nice. I like him."

"So why did he go missing for so long?"

"He won't tell me, says that's up to my mother."

Ansel chuckled, knowing the likelihood of that happening. "Guess he doesn't know her too well."

"Nope. He actually thinks there's a chance she might agree to see him."

"Really?"

"Yeah, wants me to ask her."

"Have you?"

I looked at Ansel. "I haven't even told her I've seen him yet. But she's in Chicago anyway. Won't be back until Thursday or Friday."

"That ought to be a fun conversation."

I could see he sympathized, but by then I didn't care what my mother thought of my visiting Mr. Mulvaney. There was nothing she could do about it. Her father was nothing like she had described. He was a nice old guy. "I wouldn't tell her at all except he wants to see her so badly."

"About what?"

"He doesn't want to talk about it." Ansel laughed. I did, too. "I guess my family is pretty good at that."

"I wasn't thinking of your family."

I didn't ask him who he meant, because I suspected he meant me. But what good would it have done to talk about what had happened in the cemetery? I knew how Ansel felt about me, and I knew how he didn't feel. I looked at my watch. "Mr. Kinsey's going to be wondering where you are."

Ansel tied his sneaker. "Yeah, I better go."

I stood up and put my bag over my shoulder.

Ansel extended his hand for me to help him up. I smiled and gave him a pull. He rose and let out a long sigh, sounding exhausted. I waited for him to release my hand, but he didn't. He stood with me, looking down the street, as if he couldn't remember which way he was supposed to go. "Listen," he said, "don't let this stuff get to you." I nodded, knowing he meant all the grownups' secrets. "You'll never figure them out anyway."

"I know," I said, and he squeezed my hand. I wished we could walk down the street that way, my hand in his, like I was special to him, more than someone to talk to.

He let go of my hand and walked alongside me. We were only a block from Sarah's house now. "Can I tell you something?" he said. "I mean I don't want you to get mad at me."

I said, "Sure," thinking he was going to tell me not to go see Mr. Mulvaney.

"You're a pretty good kisser. I mean for someone who hasn't done much of it." For a second, I thought he was being sarcastic. I felt ashamed, thought of the things I'd learned to do in Chicago, wondered if it had showed. "I liked it," he said. It was the last thing I expected him to say. He had seemed so eager to have it over with. I figured it didn't work for him at all.

"I didn't think you did," I told him.

"That's what I was afraid of. No. I just felt bad, because I know you don't do that stuff."

He wasn't kidding. He really thought I was innocent.

"You shouldn't feel bad," I said. "I liked it, too." My face was burning hot, as if he really was the first boy I'd ever kissed. I was so thrilled I felt dopey.

We reached Sarah's house and he asked if he could come in with me, but I reminded him that he had to get to Kinsey's.

"I don't want to go there."

"You never want to go, but you have to."

He shifted his bookbag, glanced down the block. "Okay. Well, keep me posted about Brooklyn, all right?" I told him I would, but he waited some more, as if that wasn't really what he wanted to say. I climbed the front steps and rang Sarah's doorbell, and he headed for the street. When Sarah opened the door, I turned one last time. He was still looking back at me.

twelve

The trip to Brooklyn seemed shorter that day, but it wasn't. It was just that I knew my way by then. I still felt like a foreigner, someone who didn't know the rules, but I liked being there. There were so many people, so much going on. So different from home. In our house, the three of us were like ghosts, wandering in from some other realm, without a clue how to be real anymore.

I knew which block was Clover's. I didn't have to look at the street signs. The blocks didn't all look the same to me anymore. Clover's had a dry cleaner on the corner, with signs that bragged about three-hour service. But no one I'd seen around here bothered much with creases. A sign on the door said it was closed on Tuesdays. I couldn't believe I'd met Clover only a week before.

Sarah didn't understand why I liked going to Brooklyn. When I described Mr. Mulvaney's drawings, how beautiful they were, she looked at me just the way Ansel had, as if something beautiful and fine couldn't come from a place like this, from people like Mr. Mulvaney. She didn't say those things. She just looked baffled. She agreed that the drawing of my mom was good, but she still resisted. When I pressed her, she insisted that her mother didn't work with artists in Brooklyn; it wasn't her territory. But I knew that wasn't true. She had several clients in New York, and at least one of them was in Brooklyn. "Anyway," Sarah said, "how do you think your mother would react if she found out my mom was representing her father?" I had no answer to that one. Mrs. Richardson and my mom weren't exactly friends, but their paths crossed quite a bit. They were both on the Princeton University Art Museum gala committee. But my mother was my problem, and I was sure that once Sarah saw more of Mr. Mulvaney's drawings she'd feel differently. She'd see that this was someone her mother should meet.

I got to Clover's building and headed upstairs, careful not to rely on the rickety banister. I found her apartment door, but sounds of children laughing and running came from inside. I stepped back, checked the door. 6B. I knew this was the right apartment. I rang the bell. Moments passed, then I heard what sounded like someone working her way through the kids' playing, scolding them mildly in Spanish.

The voice reached the door, opened it only enough to look out at me. A young woman. She seemed accustomed to handling unwelcome callers. "Who you want?" she said in a heavy Spanish accent.

"I'm sorry," I said. "I was looking for Deirdre Lynch. I must have the wrong floor."

"Deedrah? No Deedrah here," she said.

"Clover, I mean." The woman relaxed her hold on the door. I could see a corner of the old Magnavox in the living room, and I found myself smiling.

"Clover. Yes. You wait," the woman said, smiling at me as if at a child who'd finally found the right words. She closed the door softly.

Almost immediately, the door opened a little again and looking up at me through the space was the flawless round, brown face of a little girl with dark, serious eyes. I smiled. The girl didn't, and slammed the door. It opened yet again. Another beautiful dark face, even younger, appeared in the crack. "Boo," he said. I laughed, and giggles overtook the boy as Clover reached the doorway behind him.

"You've come then. Good," she said.

I smiled. I couldn't get used to these greetings. They were more like commentaries. But she seemed pleased enough to see me. "I was afraid I had the wrong apartment."

"We have a full house here this afternoon," Clover said. "I wasn't expecting you so early." I'd clearly caught her off guard.

"I got an earlier train, and no delays this time."

The young woman disappeared into one of the bedrooms off the long hall. Clover took me to the kitchen. "Did you meet Delores? That's my neighbor," she said. "She works in that Spanish banana store across the street. I watch the kids for her sometimes. Hector, he's the owner, he gives her a break on the groceries."

"She speaks English?"

"She manages well enough. She's a good woman, Morgan." Clover raised her voice over the music coming from the room Delores was in. "Come in here, Delores," she called. "Come meet Morgan."

There was a pause, then footsteps behind us. I turned in my chair. "Delores, this is Morgan, my dear friend come all the way from Princeton, New Jersey."

Delores said hello, guarded. I smiled and greeted her. She was tall, thin. Over her jeans she wore old woolen leg warmers. Her sweater was studded with pills, and she kept her hands in the deep pockets. She seemed shy but interested, as if she knew some secret about me. "Hello. Very nice," she said.

"You live in this building, too?" I said.

"Yes, my place is downstairs, near your grandfather's." I winced at her calling him that, hoped Clover hadn't noticed.

Clover called to the children, who appeared immediately. Maybe they'd been listening outside the whole time. The girl came alongside her mother, who put a hand on the girl's shoulder, pulled her close. The boy ran past her to the table. The girl and her mother swayed to the music coming from the other room.

"I like that music," I said.

"Abriendo Caminos. You know them?"

"No, but it sounds good."

"Fusion," she said, although it took me a second to decipher her accent.

"Come here to me, John," said Clover. "John, this is Morgan. Say hello." He gave me a tiny hello, then a smile that pulled at me. "Say hello, Tina." The girl just stared at me, the side of her face pressed against her mother's hip. "Tina takes her time gettin' to know folks," said Clover. "Come sit down, Delores. Come talk with Morgan. You remember me telling you about the mansion of a house she's got. Why, even the washing machine has a room of its own."

"I have been to New Jersey," Delores told me.

"You have?"

"Yes. West New York."

"I've never been there."

"We go dance there."

"Really?" I said.

"We used to go, yes." Her voice got a little soft, sort of sad.

"Delores loves to dance," Clover sighed, as if she admired this passion in her, shared it.

"And you, too," Delores said to Clover. "Don't pretend you don't."

"Those days are long past."

"You can dance," said Delores, and she put a hand on Clover's waist and held her arm. "I showed you."

"Ah, we don't have time for this," Clover told her, but Delores moved to the Latin beat, sang some of the words. The children giggled as Clover laughed and let Delores move with her.

Then I heard him laughing over the music. "So this is what you do all day?" said Mr. Mulvaney, chuckling. He stood in the doorway, his arms filled with grocery bags.

"She's a bad influence," Clover said.

The children were happy to see him, and they came close, expecting something. He put the bags on the table, reached into the pockets of his jacket, one after another, tsking in exaggerated frustration, as if he couldn't find what he wanted. Finally, he reached deep into his pants pocket, made the change jingle. He pulled out a handful of coins and candies wrapped in silver foil and opened his palm as the children took their prizes.

"She's a great one for holding out on people," Mr. Mulvaney said to Delores. "When I met her she told me she couldn't dance a lick."

"I told you no such thing. Why would I? You never wanted to take me to a ceili."

Delores began to gather her things. "Where are you headed?" Mr. Mulvaney asked her.

"Just want to let the kids play outside before it gets too dark."

"It was a pleasure meeting you," I said.

"My pleasure," she said, and Clover walked her and the kids to the door. They talked in urgent whispers, and I couldn't make out what they were saying.

"What's a ceili?" I asked Mr. Mulvaney.

"A dance," he explained.

"How did you meet each other?"

"Tell her, Terence," said Clover, returning to the kitchen, her arms folded across her chest like a proctor at an exam.

"Ah . . . bejesus . . . Clover," said Mr. Mulvaney, his body sinking into a chair as if he'd already failed the test. "You know I'm no good at that stuff."

"As I thought," said Clover, exasperated.

"Wait," said Mr. Mulvaney, raising his hand, determined to prove himself. "It was cold. Christmas time. I was just moved in. You told me where to get shaving cream."

"Shoelaces."

"There you have it," he agreed, hands resting on his knees, ready to move on now to easier topics.

"But that was not the first time we met."

"Sure it was, woman."

"Sure it was not."

"If this is the way you're going to be, then I'm done with questions," he said, slapping his knees. But the resolve was half-hearted. I suspected he was mostly enjoying this.

"Maybe that's just as well, since you've got the memory of a sotted cow," she said.

"I've put up with this for too many years, Deirdre Lynch. You're as stubborn and thick as ever. Why, if I so much as say my name, you want to see my driver's license before you'll admit I'm right."

"You lost that years ago, remember? Driving home drunk from Callahan's birthday party all the way out in Queens. And you seem to have a confused notion of who puts up with whom."

"Tell me about the dancing," I said. "Where did you go dancing?"

But Clover went on, hardly missing a beat. "To set the record straight," she said, addressing me, "we met on the stairs of this building while I was carrying down the trash."

"Really?" I said, trying not to giggle.

"He had the good manners to offer to carry the bag for me. I'll give him that."

"That? That you consider our first meeting?" Mr. Mulvaney crossed his arms. "Lookin' at your green eyes over a bag of garbage? What about our walk, with the snow piled as high as the parking meters all the way to the park? And the moon big as Cuchulain's fist in the black night? Tell me you don't remember that."

"I do, Terence." There was a funny sound from Clover, like she had to catch her breath. "And now we're losing everything," she said in a small voice. I was confused at this, but Clover caught herself and cut off my question. "This fine granddaughter of yours is our angel. She's come just in time." I didn't understand what she meant.

"I was wondering about your drawings," I said. "They're so beautiful. Are there a lot more of them?"

"They're like bad pennies," Mr. Mulvaney said. "They turn up everywhere."

"I'd love to see more of them."

"I have one in my bedroom," said Clover. "Would you like to see it?"

"Sure," I said, and followed her into the hall, where a door led into a small room with rosy wallpaper and gauzy curtains and doilies on all the furniture. The room was close; the air in it smelled faintly of lavender. She pointed to the wall on our right as we entered, and there was a framed landscape, in the same grays as the other drawings I'd seen, the same delicate detail.

"Dingle Bay," she said.

In the background, huge majestic cliffs jutted up from the water, and in the foreground, in the center, there were a girl and two dogs waiting by a gate. The wind lifted her hair and she pulled a jacket close around her. There was a sense of something about to happen, or of something that never would happen again. "Who is that?" I said.

"He won't tell me. Probably just someone he dreamed up."

"It's so beautiful."

"It brings me good dreams." She turned and I followed her out to the kitchen.

"Mr. Mulvaney, that's so beautiful. You're very good. Do you ever show your pictures anywhere or sell them?"

He only laughed.

"I know someone who could do that for you. My girlfriend's mother does it for a living. She finds buyers for artists' work.

Sometimes she gets the local restaurants and coffee shops to display the art so people can see it. Sometimes they even buy it. Her artists have even had shows in galleries."

"Don't be silly, child. I'm just a dabbler."

"But yours is nicer than some of the work she represents. One guy makes stuff out of rubber bands and old CD cases."

He chuckled. "I went to the Museum of Modern Art last year, and folks were gathered round an old pair of sneakers sitting on a wooden chair in a corner. Remember, Clover? We went looking around for the barefoot kid."

"Mrs. Richardson, that's my girlfriend's mom, she says artists like that want to make people see things in new ways."

"Sneakers, for heaven's sake," said Clover. "If you've seen one, haven't you seen 'em all?"

"I'd like to show Mrs. Richardson some of your drawings. May I take some home with me?"

Mr. Mulvaney grinned, exchanged a look with Clover. "I'd best be dustin' off that beret."

Clover laughed.

"Did you show the one I gave you to your mother?" said Mr. Mulvaney.

"No, she's still in Chicago."

"So you haven't talked to her?"

"About her seeing him," Clover explained, but she didn't have to. I knew what he had meant.

"Not yet." She could see I didn't want to do it. Mr. Mulvaney sighed, as if he'd expected no more than this and we all needed to move on to something else.

"It's very important, Morgan," said Clover. "We have to talk with her."

The alarm in her voice was barely disguised. And it confused me. This wasn't the way Mr. Mulvaney had described it. He had made it seem as if he just wanted a chance to talk with her. I figured he wanted to apologize. But Clover made it sound like something urgent and scary.

"It's a shame they couldn't have given her a decent Christian name," Mr. Mulvaney said, clearly wanting to change the subject. It took me a second to realize he was talking about me.

"Truly," said Clover.

"Let me do that at least for you," said the old man.

"That would be a fine thing," Clover agreed.

"She's certainly got fight in her," he said to Clover.

"And a will."

"Good. Then we should keep the M, after her undaunted mother."

"Something royal."

"Indeed. We'll call her Maud," he said.

"There's a grand name for you," Clover said to me.

"For me?"

"Yes," said Mr. Mulvaney. "For you. A name worthy of an Irish woman, not a trust company."

"After Maud Gonne MacBride," said Clover. "She was a legend in her own time in Ireland, a woman who fought for the poor."

"Maud," I whispered. I liked the sound of it, and I liked the way I fit here with these two. They made me feel like I mattered to them—even though I could see they were embarrassed with me, still guarded, as if they had to keep their affection in check for fear it wouldn't be returned.

"Thank you," I told him.

He smiled.

"But I wish you'd tell me what's wrong," I said. "Why is it so important for you to talk to my mother?" He reached for his cigarettes, then caught himself, remembering Clover didn't allow him to smoke in her apartment.

"She's the only one can—" Clover started.

"There's no need to go into that. That's for the grownups to sort out," said Mr. Mulvaney.

"But maybe if I could explain to my mother, she would—"

"It's not for you to be explainin' any of this."

I wished they would tell me what was wrong. I was afraid for them. I didn't know what I could say to my mother that would convince her to meet with them. If I knew what it was about, maybe I'd at least have a chance. "I'll ask her to come here with me."

They looked at me, wanting more.

"Maybe she can come with me after school, at the end of the week when she gets back from Chicago."

"Grand," said Clover, as if it was all set.

thirteen

Mr. Mulvaney gave me four drawings—two landscapes, another of a narrow street that he said was in Cork, and one of a man sitting at a table near a window in a small room, drinking coffee. They were all beautiful, but I liked the Cork street the best. It looked like early morning on a gray, overcast day. The buildings seemed to lean in, making the street even narrower, insular. A woman in a doorway stood staring, suspicious, as if she'd stepped outside just to see what you were up to.

I took them to Sarah's as soon as I got back, but her mother wasn't home yet. I could see Sarah liked them, but she still didn't want to show them to her mother. She said she was worried about how my mother would react if she found out. There was no mystery about that. She'd be furious. And I didn't care. But Sarah did. To her, it could only mean trouble.

This wasn't the first time I'd noticed how much like her parents Sarah was sometimes. She could be crazy, do some outrageous things, but she was hypersensitive to what people might think. And that applied to everything: her grades, her hemlines, the cars her parents drove, even the restaurants they chose. People who had money in Princeton, or at least an image to protect, didn't just dread scandal or embarrassment; they saw themselves as part of some gentile elite with the best jobs and the best degrees, and they kept their distance from anything that might smell of bad taste or take them down a peg. Sarah's mother was bound to ask what my connection was to Mr. Mulvaney, and it was becoming obvious that Sarah thought that keeping him a secret wasn't a bad idea.

But she came through for me. In first period Wednesday morning, she told me she'd shown the drawings to her mother and she liked them. But Mrs. Richardson said she couldn't judge from just four drawings; she needed more. Sarah didn't tell her mom who Mr. Mulvaney actually was, just that he was a distant relative of mine. I was thrilled, but I had to figure out how I was going to get her more drawings. Mr. Mulvaney had told me some of them were in frames, the ones he'd "fussed over" in charcoal. They'd be too heavy to take on the train.

I looked for Sarah when school let out that day to talk with her about it, but we didn't get to talk very long. From the foot of the school steps, I spotted my mother's car.

"Look, Sarah. That's my mother's BMW."

"At the corner?" said Sarah. "But I thought she was in Chicago."

"So did I."

"I wonder if your dad told her you went to Brooklyn yesterday?" said Sarah.

"He said he wouldn't." I headed toward the car, making my way through the kids who stood in groups here and there along the tree-lined sidewalk. Sarah followed.

"Hey, Morgan," Ansel called. I stopped to wait, watched him break away from a small group and come toward me, Susan attached to his hip.

"Are we still on for later?" he said.

Susan said hi. I did the same, avoiding her eyes. They were very blue, very bright. She had Ansel's sweater on, the neckline stretched and slanted, exposing a freckled shoulder and the strap of a bright pink bra. I looked at Ansel, confused.

"Are we still on for tonight?" He stepped away from Susan and moved close to me. "To work on the paper?" he said.

"Oh, right. Sure," I said, trying to sound normal, but I didn't know where I'd be that night. Maybe Brooklyn.

"My dad found some books we can take a look at," he said, leaning toward me. "About the Depression."

"Okay," I said, and moved away. "But I have to go."

"What's the hurry?" he called after me.

"My mom's here."

I could see he thought I was in trouble. "Morgan. Morgan, wait. Can I help?"

"Not really," I called back.

"See you tonight."

"I'll come with you," Sarah said, catching up.

"Better not," I said, and she stayed put. She must have known this wouldn't be fun to watch.

My mom was still searching the crowd, couldn't see me approaching yet. I didn't wave, but I saw her eyes brighten as I got close.

My mother leaned across to open the door for me, and I got in. "Hi," I said, not very warmly. "You're home early."

"We had it pretty much sold by Tuesday." She put her arms around me. The embrace was quick, but her look lingered. I was accustomed to these looks when she returned from her trips. It was as if she was searching for things she might have missed while she was away—something different about my hair, a look in my eyes that wasn't there before. "They can handle the rest without me," she said, turning the car on. "I'm glad you spotted me. I was about to call your cell."

I didn't say anything, didn't want to tell her that I checked the corner every day for her BMW—every day since that time six months before, when Grandpa went into the hospital for the first time. The car had simply appeared that day—unplanned—and we went for ice cream and a long walk, for no particular reason except that I knew my mother was afraid. She was about to lose one of the few people who meant something to her. And I could see that she had no idea how to handle it.

I watched her at the hospital, trying all her usual ways of keeping chaos away: getting on the phone to the doctors, arranging for a different room, insisting on more tests, leaving instructions at the nurses' station. But when there were no more decisions to make or orders to give and she had to sit by Grandpa's bedside, she didn't want to take his hand. He reached for her, but she fluffed his pillow instead, asked him what he needed. "Give me your hand," he said. And he took her hand in both of his and I watched her face, wondering if she'd lose control, cry great deep sobs that would make the moment seem like a scene in some sentimental movie.

But she didn't. She sat there beside him, awkwardly, until he smiled at her and said something about Blumenthal, the dog that belonged to the Farrells down the street. He used to walk the dog for them early in the morning. "Have they found someone to walk the dog?" he said.

Mom shook her head no. "Mrs. Farrell said she'll do it herself until you're better."

"Well, they'd better go ahead and find someone."

"No need for that," she said stiffly. That was as close as they got to talking about what was about to happen to them both.

I treasured our ice cream day. We talked about nothing in particular—clothes, teachers, a new shade of nail polish. I hoped there would be more afternoons like that one, and I checked the corner for the car every day. But it was never there.

We had stepped back that day into the way it used to be. We had done things together, a movie once in a while, a card game. But not long after we moved to Chicago, my mother began to seem different, preoccupied. I blamed it on her new job, on having to travel more, then later, once we got to New Jersey, on Grandpa's illness. The change was so gradual that I didn't see it at first. The new things in my own life—the time I spent with Ansel and Sarah—helped me pretend that I was the one changing.

Things changed with my father as well. He would be gone for part of a weekend—off to some observatory or conference—and come back sad, quiet. By then, my parents had stopped having coffee together in the morning. The smell of it filling the house had always awakened me at five o'clock, and I would drift back to sleep to the sound of their voices in the kitchen. Things never went back to normal. My mother got her coffee on her way to work.

"I'd like to talk to you, Morgan," Mom said, "instead of going straight home, I mean." She pulled away and headed toward the avenue.

"Fine."

My mother drove for a bit. We listened to the news on the radio, and Mom called my attention to the houses decorated for Halloween. She tried to keep things casual, but I could tell by the way she gripped the steering wheel that she was tense. Finally, she pulled onto a side street and parked under a large elm. "Morgan," she said, turning off the car, "about this business with Clover."

"Dad told you?" I said, but I didn't look at her.

"This morning. He said you've gone there several times, that I should get the rest from you."

What did she want me to say? Did she really think I was going to pretend I'd never found the woman? Stuff everything back into its hiding place for her?

"Yes, I go there. What about it?"

She raised her hand, as if to calm me. "I'm not upset with you."

I didn't believe her. "You don't mind?"

"I didn't say that, but if it's what you feel you need to do, I won't stop you."

The truth was she couldn't stop me. And she knew it. "I like her," I said.

"What is she like?"

"She's a little strange, but she's pretty funny. The way she says things. These odd expressions."

"Irishisms. They seep into every conversation. Grandma had her share. Took me years to get rid of mine."

I didn't want to say anymore about it. She would only find a way to spoil it all.

"I need you to try to understand something," she said. "You have every right to talk to her. I was wrong to keep secrets. Your father warned me what would come of it. I'm just asking you to understand that this is very difficult for me."

"I'm trying to understand," I told her. "But I don't. Not at all." I looked out the window at the empty street. "Clover doesn't lie to me. She doesn't pretend."

"Everyone pretends. It's just a matter of what it is they're hiding."

I turned to look at her. "She doesn't pretend about your father."

"What do you mean?"

"She doesn't pretend that he's dead."

She closed her eyes tightly, as if she wanted to shut out what would have to come next. "You've seen him then?" she said, her voice barely audible.

"Yes."

"Oh, God," she sighed.

"I met him on Saturday at Clover's, and the next day we went to the warehouse where he works—"

But she couldn't listen. "I don't want to hear about this."

"Mom, he's a nice man. Just a nice old man."

She cut me off with a look, as if to make sure there would be no question about who Mr. Mulvaney really was. "I don't know what kind of man you met or what kind of man Clover has convinced you he is. But the man I remember couldn't keep it together long enough to come through for anyone. Ever. He always had an excuse—some of them were actually convincing—but the real reason was always the same: his drinking. That's what came first, before everything and everyone else." She got quiet, took a long breath, tried to calm herself.

"He's not drinking anymore," I said. "That's all over. I don't understand why you can't—"

"That doesn't matter. That's not what this is about."

"I'm just telling you he was nice to me. He—"

"These people are not interested in you, Morgan. They've got a whole other agenda, and it's not about you."

"Why are you saying that? I don't understand."

"I know you don't," she said, her voice softer now. "He's already got you convinced that he cares about you. Don't kid yourself. He's gotten himself into some kind of trouble and he's using you to get to me."

"You're wrong about him," I insisted, but I'd asked myself the same thing. I still wondered about his call that night, when he suddenly changed his mind about seeing me a second time. "You don't know anything about him."

"I know he doesn't care anything about you, that's for sure."

"How can you say that?"

"Because if he did, we'd know it by now. He would have asked to meet you." She looked away.

It hurt to hear that, but I pushed it away. He must have had a reason. "Do you know he's really talented?" I said. "He makes beautiful drawings."

"He was always doodling."

"Well, he doesn't just doodle. He's good. Even Mrs. Richardson thinks so."

The look on her face made me want to get out of the car. "What does *she* know about this?"

"We showed Mrs. Richardson his drawings. She may represent him."

"Represent him? How dare you? How dare you get Brenda Richardson involved in this?"

"Oh, don't fret, Mother. Your place in Princeton society is safe. You don't have to worry about anybody knowing your father is in the wrong tax bracket."

"It isn't about that."

"No? Sure sounds that way."

"My father is none of anyone's business, Morgan. And don't you speak to me that way."

I stayed quiet and she sat rigid, as if there could be no other truth but hers, no other side to Terence Mulvaney. But the man in her head wasn't anything like the man I had met. Why couldn't she just give him a chance? "Wasn't he ever kind to you?" I said finally. "Don't you remember anything good about him?"

She didn't answer for a long time. She looked out the window at the kids walking home from school, then down at her hands on the wheel. Finally, she said something, in a voice barely audible. "He read to me," she said. "Early in the morning, before anyone else was awake." She took a deep breath, ready to put the whole business away, then started the car. I assumed the subject was closed, but as we moved onto the main street, she said something odd. "Was he happy to see you?"

"Yes," I insisted. "He's very kind, and sometimes he's funny. Just like Clover, he—"

"That's all I wanted to know."

"There's one more thing," I said, only because I promised I would. "He wants to know if he can talk to you."

"Did he ask you that, or did Clover?"

"He did. He asked me to find out if there was any chance that could happen."

Her answer came before I finished speaking. "There isn't."

"Mom, it's really important to them. I think there's something wrong, something they need your help with."

"That's not news."

"But Mom—"

"Morgan, don't ask me again. Please. Stop this," she said. So I did, because I knew she was too twisted up to listen to reason. She didn't want to know what was happening to these people, any more than she really wanted to know what was happening to me.

fourteen

The roads were still wet from the rain. It started before school ended, but it was mostly over by the time we got to Brooklyn. It took forever to get there in mid-day traffic, and it seemed odd going by car. Dad did most of the talking, although he avoided going over the obvious again: why Mr. Mulvaney and Clover wanted to talk to Mom so badly and how I was going to explain why she wouldn't do it. When I called Clover to tell her I was coming, I didn't exactly make clear that it would be without my mother. Instead I was bringing my father, hoping if I came with a grownup—any grownup—in tow, they'd stop the nonsense and tell me what was wrong. They obviously needed money. Why they thought my mother would give them any was baffling. I wasn't sure my father would either. The only way I could think of to help them was to find a way to sell Mr. Mulvaney's drawings.

It didn't take much convincing to get my father to take me to Brooklyn. Maybe he wanted a closer look at these people I'd been spending so much time with. Solving the enigma of the black holes could wait one more day. I had told him Mom refused to come to Brooklyn. He didn't offer to try to persuade her, said he wasn't the most effective lobbyist with her these days. Like I hadn't noticed. So mostly Dad and I talked about the drawings. He asked me what size the frames might be, about fitting them into the trunk. Of course, I had no idea.

When we reached Clover's building, she was waiting outside. The sunlight made the wet pavement glisten. We pulled over to the curb, and Dad looked at her, took a long, weary breath. "Go ahead," he said. "I'll go park the car."

I got out quickly, climbed the stoop, and watched the car pull away. "Let's get inside," Clover whispered, as if the sunlight could protect us from only so much. Inside, the hall was dark, the smells strong. "I take it she wouldn't come?" she said.

I shook my head no. "My father brought me," I told her. "Maybe you can talk with him?"

"He's a stubborn man, Maud." She meant Mr. Mulvaney, of course.

Dad opened the door to the vestibule so slowly and cautiously that only the cool air he had let in made us turn. His grip on the door handle was tentative, as if it wasn't a solid door at all but some prop on a movie set that he had to treat with care.

"Clover," I said. "This is my dad."

"John Lindstrum," my father said, offering his hand.

"A pleasure, sir." Clover shook his hand as if she were sealing a deal. "I hope you didn't have too much traffic," she said, turning to lead us up the first flight.

"Not much at all."

"There's just too many cars on the road nowadays," she called over her shoulder. "Families have two and three."

"I'm afraid we're guilty there," Dad said, the expression on his face now registering the odors in the hall. "Schedules and all."

"Schedules, of course," said Clover, and I could tell she was holding back, trying to be polite.

At the fifth-floor landing, she stopped and headed down the dim hall. "But this is only the fifth," I said, making the turn for the next flight.

"No," Clover said, beckoning me to follow. "You want to get the drawings, don't you? They're in your grand . . . in Mr. Mulvaney's place."

"His place is on this floor?" said Dad.

"Right here," said Clover, already knocking.

"Clover, is that you?" Mr. Mulvaney's voice seemed to come from the far end of the apartment.

"Now, who else would it be? And I've got Maud here," she told him matter-of-factly.

"Maud? Wait," he said, as if he feared I'd be gone before he could get to the door, "I'm coming."

"Maud?" my father said.

"I'll explain later," I whispered.

In a moment the locks and latches were undone and the big man stood in the doorway. He glanced briefly at me, then settled his gaze on my dad. "This is John Lindstrum, Maud's father," said Clover.

"Pleasure to meet you, Mr. Mulvaney," Dad said, extending his hand.

Mr. Mulvaney looked at Dad's face, then down at their handshake, as if this simple exchange was something he'd forgotten how to do. "Good to see you. Good to see you at last," Mr. Mulvaney said. He wasn't just being polite; he was excited. Dad nodded in agreement. I could see he was curious about Mr. Mulvaney, but his look was mixed with something else I couldn't read.

"Come in," said Mr. Mulvaney. "Come in." We moved into the apartment's long, narrow entryway, and Mr. Mulvaney and Clover exchanged a look. "When do we see her?" he said in a low voice. She raised her hand in a gesture that told him the answer would have to wait. "Well," he said, turning to me. "Were you this tall when I saw you last?" He patted my shoulder, maybe self-conscious about doing any more than that with my dad there. "I'm glad you've come," he said.

The rooms of the apartment were laid out almost exactly like Clover's, but unlike hers, the living room, at least, was nearly empty. It had very little furniture and almost nothing on the walls except a few of his drawings. A single window was covered only in a thin, sheer curtain that let the light go wherever it pleased. Sunshine had muted the flowers in the thin carpet, now all but indistinguishable from the leaves. Across the room, a large radio sat on a shaky snack table below a framed copy of some sort of proclamation whose lettering I couldn't make out from where I was standing. Hanging above the apartment door was a small Celtic cross.

"Pull up a chair," said Mr. Mulvaney, but there was only a couch and a low, straight-backed wooden chair near the window. Dad took the chair, and I sat down in the center of the couch, sinking quickly into its unexpected depth. While I struggled to right myself, on each side of me Clover and Mr. Mulvaney accepted the couch's overbearing embrace with grace.

"This is quite a surprise," said Mr. Mulvaney. I said nothing. I was afraid he thought we'd come with a message from my mom or something. "It's grand to see you. Grand."

No one knew what to say. Mr. Mulvaney coughed long and hard, and I could swear I heard Clover humming. Dad sat with his back too straight, his hands on his knees. Twice I saw him start to reach inside his jacket for a cigarette, then think better of it. He was surely desperate for one. He gestured toward the cigarette butts in the ashtray nearby. "Would you mind if I smoked?" he said.

Mr. Mulvaney raised his hand, as if in caution.

"Filthy habit," Clover said under her breath.

"Well, I don't mind personally," said Mr. Mulvaney. "I'm a smoker myself, but I've given my word that there's no smoking when Clover is here."

"Oh, of course," said Dad.

"You're welcome to step out onto the fire escape," said Mr. Mulvaney, pointing to the narrow window. "I do that now and again."

"That's very kind of you," Dad said. "I'm fine."

"So," said Clover, an effort that landed somewhere between getting things started and summing them up.

"So," said Mr. Mulvaney.

"Mr. Lindstrum here teaches at the Princeton University," said Clover.

"Does he now?"

Dad nodded eagerly, clearly relieved that someone at last had found something to say.

"He's an astrophysicist," Clover said grandly.

"You don't say."

"Isn't that right, Mr. Lindstrum?" said Clover, as if settling an argument.

"Yes, yes. That's right."

Another silence followed, with Clover and Mr. Mulvaney apparently waiting for more and Dad still stiff and ill at ease. "And what exactly is involved?" said Mr. Mulvaney tentatively. "In that line of work, I mean?"

"There's a tremendous amount of research," said Dad, eager to fill the silence. "Right now I'm spending a great deal of time on gravitational forces, dark matter. My field is theoretical physics, you see."

"I see," said Mr. Mulvaney almost as if he did.

Dad seemed to be at a loss for how to explain.

"Dad, tell them about the Andromeda Galaxy," I said.

"Ah, yes, yes. Truly fascinating," he said, grateful for the topic. "This is not a project of mine, I should say, but I've been following the work of some physicists at the University of Toronto who have managed to track the collision that will inevitably take place between our galaxy—the Milky Way—and the Andromeda Galaxy."

"A collision, did you say?" said Clover, clearly uneasy about this news.

"Yes, a collision, an event of major proportions to say the least."

"Well," said Mr. Mulvaney, "I'm glad to hear someone's staying on top of it."

"The galaxies will definitely merge, you see. Right now there's a 2.2-million-light-year gap between the two galaxies, and Andromeda is closing it at about 500,000 kilometers an hour."

"How long do we have?" said Clover, a bit breathless.

"How long do we have?" Dad repeated, not seeming to understand the question.

"Yes. Before we collide?"

"Oh, yes. Well, if the Canadian Institute for Theoretical Astrophysics is correct—and I suspect it is—the merger will take place in less than three billion years."

Clover and Mr. Mulvaney needed a second to take this in. "Three billion, you say?" said Mr. Mulvaney.

"No more than that," said Dad earnestly, as if the matter were something that had been neglected far too long.

"Then there'll be time enough to say a good Act of Contrition," said Clover.

"Well, it sounds like important work you're doing," said Mr. Mulvaney, "protecting the universe and the like. I'm all for it."

"Well, thank you."

There was another silence, made all the more uncomfortable for Dad since Mr. Mulvaney had now begun to stare at him. "She resembles you a little," Mr. Mulvaney said. "Her chin. I didn't see it 'til just now."

Dad nodded.

"How did you two meet?" asked Clover. "You and Maud's mother, I mean."

"Oh." Dad cleared his throat. "We were in school together. At Yale."

"But you were already a graduate student by then, isn't that right?" said Mr. Mulvaney.

"Yes. Yes. That's correct." Dad squirmed in his narrow chair.

"Peter mentions things now and then," said Mr. Mulvaney. "He's told me about the house. Is it really that big?"

"You mean our house in Princeton?"

"Yes, tremendous lot of rooms, Peter says."

"It's certainly more house than we need. And now with Grandpa gone, it's . . . " Dad caught himself, uncomfortable about having mentioned Grandpa. Things got quiet again.

"I'm glad you came," Mr. Mulvaney said, as if we hadn't heard him the first six times.

I found myself smiling, happy to hear him say it but afraid he was not going to be glad when he realized my mother wouldn't see him.

"I guess . . . we'd like to know more about you. I understand you draw," Dad said, but Mr. Mulvaney cut him off.

"Oh, that," he said. "I don't understand what all the fuss is about."

"I have some ready for you," said Clover. "There they are." She pointed to at least half a dozen framed drawings leaning against the wall. They were covered by a blanket. A large manila envelope rested beside them. "And there are some more in the envelope."

"That's great," I said.

"Let me take those down to the car." Dad got to his feet, welcoming the excuse to get away.

"That can wait," said Mr. Mulvaney.

"I don't mind, really. I'm a little worried about the car anyway." Then he glanced at his watch, turned to me. "And Morgan, we need to be getting back," he said, though we couldn't have been there more than twenty minutes. It was obvious he wanted no part of these people. He went over to the frames and removed the blanket, lifted them to test their weight, then put them down.

"Let me help you with those," said Mr. Mulvaney, rising from the couch.

"Oh, don't get up. Please. They're not a problem. Morgan can take the envelope for me." He took a step toward Mr. Mulvaney. "A pleasure to meet you, Mr. Mulvaney," he said, his hand extended.

"I thought we might talk for a bit, the two of us," Mr. Mulvaney told him.

"Of course. Any time." Dad reached into his jacket for his notebook. He wrote his number on a page and tore it out.

Mr. Mulvaney let the paper hang there. "How about now?" he said.

I could see my father was taken off guard, but he agreed. They took the frames and stepped outside.

Clover and I sat down again. "I wish you would just tell me what's wrong," I said.

"There's nothing wrong with a man wanting to see his daughter."

"There's more to it than that. It's obvious. Can't you just tell me what it is?"

"He won't let me."

"Let you? That's ridiculous. Why won't you tell me?"

"He's asked me not to, Maud. I have to respect that."

I wished they'd show some respect for me, but I didn't say it. We sat in silence for a while until the door opened and Mr. Mulvaney came in. I could see he was not happy.

"Well, that was quick," Clover said.

"There's no point in talking to him."

"He wants to help," I said, wanting to believe that was true.

"Does your mother even know you brought him here?" Mr. Mulvaney said sharply.

"No. But he wanted to come. He wanted to meet you. You're family."

"Wanted to see what kind of slum you were taking yourself off to more like it," said Clover.

"Clover," Mr. Mulvaney scolded, then turned to me. "This is never going to be what you think. We're nothing like that."

"Nothing like what?" I said.

"Nothing like family. And you mustn't be thinkin' of us that way."

"That's pretty pathetic." I said it under my breath, but I wanted to scream it at him. He was my grandfather, someone I'd never even been allowed to know. And now he wanted me to act as if that didn't matter and never would.

"Yes," he said. "It's that."

"So that's what you want?"

That set him off. "Get your head out of your fairy tale. We're in trouble here. Is that not as plain as the nose on your face? We need answers from your mother, not art dealers and geeks with their heads in the galaxies."

"No, it isn't *plain*," I said, not realizing at first that I was yelling at him. "If you want to keep everything so damn secret, how am I supposed to help you? What am I supposed to tell her?"

He wouldn't look at me. "You'd better go."

Clover sighed and rose from the couch. "Yes," she said. "Your father's waiting."

"I'll walk her down," Mr. Mulvaney said.

"I don't need you," I said.

Clover came closer. "Now, child," she said, and hugged me, warmly this time. And I could feel in it something she couldn't say. But I was fed up with them, and I said goodbye to her.

Mr. Mulvaney said nothing on the way downstairs. From the front steps, we could see my father waiting for me in his car. It was parked by a hydrant near the corner, half a block away. It was easy to spot—there weren't many cars less than ten years old on that street—but still he waved his arm out the window when he saw us.

"Goodbye," I told Mr. Mulvaney, and headed toward my father's car. In a step or two, he was at my side.

"Hold on now," he said. He took my arm and we walked more slowly. "It's a tough situation, Maud. It's not the kind of thing to burden a child with," he said. I didn't answer. I was so tired of hearing everybody's excuses for lying. "It has nothing to do with how I feel about you. Don't doubt that for a minute." We stopped a little ways from the car. The people around us moved forward when the light turned green, but we just stood there. I looked at him, wishing he could see me as a real person, someone who could help him if he'd let me. He touched my hair. The gesture made me lightheaded. I felt nervous, insubstantial, as if the wind might scatter us both at any moment. "There's nothing I'd like more than to be your grandfather," he said. "But things are a little crazy right now. So you're going to have to bear with me. Can you do that?"

"I'll try. Yes."

"All right then. Here's what I want you to do. And it won't be easy." I knew what was coming. "You must convince your mother to call me. Can you do that?"

"Mr. Mulvaney, you don't understand. She—"

"Maud," he said, as if I were being cowardly and he couldn't bear to see that. "I said it would not be easy."

"I'll try," I said, knowing that I'd have to find some other way.

fifteen

When I got to Mr. Kinsey's store after school the next day, the old man was doing his books. From the amount of time he spent on his ledgers, I figured his little business generated as much accounting work as IBM. He worked on them every Friday without fail.

"Morgan, how are you?" he said. He straightened himself slowly to see me better.

"I'm okay. How are you?" I said, hoping conversation wasn't going to be required. I was nervous about seeing Ansel. I hadn't seen much of him—at least not without Susan on his arm—since Monday, when he'd walked me to Sarah's. Every time I saw him with Susan I was tempted to stroll by and ask him if that offer to go for a drive was still good. We could talk more about how my mouth-to-mouth skills were coming along. I wanted to talk with him about Mr. Mulvaney, but I just couldn't handle seeing him alone. Sarah told me she'd meet me at the store, so I made a point of getting there a little late. My father and I had dropped the drawings off at her house when we got back from Brooklyn, and Sarah had promised to show them to her mother as soon as she got home. I was desperate to find out what she thought.

Mr. Kinsey had a big smile on his face. He liked me. "I'm just fine. We had a busy day here," he said, and tapped his forehead, remembering something. "I'm glad you came by. I've got your father's notebooks." He reached under the counter, brought out two pocket-sized leather notebooks, the ones my father carried around in his suit jackets all the time, filling them with scribbles about force fields and intergalactic resonance. Mr. Kinsey ordered them special for him regularly.

"Great. I'll give them to him. Thanks, Mr. Kinsey."

"Ansel is in the back, eager to be rescued, I'm sure," he said and winked at me.

I found Ansel elbow-deep in a box of fountain pens. "Hi," he said.

There was no sign of Sarah. "Hi," I said. "Where's Sarah?"

Ansel was wearing the Nike T-shirt Sarah's mother had given him on his birthday, the one he described as her attempt to raise his commercial consciousness a notch. "Beats me."

"She said she had to run an errand for her mother, but that shouldn't have taken long." I found a spot on the floor between some boxes. "She'll be here soon."

"That figures," he said.

"What's that supposed to mean?"

"Nothing in particular," Ansel said, returning to sorting the pens. "Just that I hardly ever see you anymore unless you're with Sarah."

"What difference does that make?"

"Some."

"What?" I said, even though I knew what he meant. It was obvious I'd been avoiding him. Maybe he missed talking with me, but not for the same reasons I did. And I had to face that.

"I can't talk to you when Sarah's here. You know. About stuff."

"Oh, you mean about Susan?" I reached into the box beside me, poked at the miniature staplers and tiny pencil sharpeners. "What's to talk about anymore anyway? We know what happens next. You must be well into stage two by now, right? She's still kind of cute, but you're getting a little bored. By Thanksgiving—or maybe even Halloween if she's not careful—you'll want my thoughts on how to dump her—gently, of course."

"You make it sound like my only problem in life is girls."

"Sorry. I forgot about Phillies tickets." I stopped myself, realizing I might sound angry and I had no way to explain that without giving myself away.

"You're mad at me, aren't you?"

"I am not mad at you," I said, but not quite calmly enough.

"Listen, what happened at the cemetery—"

"It was nothing."

"That's not what I'd call it," he said.

"I don't need to hear you say you're sorry again, okay?" And I didn't need to hear him claim he liked it again, especially when I had to see him against the lockers with his hand on Susan's hip every day. I picked up a fistful of jumbo clips, wishing I could throw them across the room.

"But—"

"You don't have to explain."

"Yes, I do. You're upset."

"I am, but not about you." I let the jumbo clips clatter back into the box.

"What's wrong?" he said, getting up to sit down beside me.

"I went to Brooklyn again. They're desperate to talk to my mother. I asked if she would, but it's no go. So I brought my dad."

"To Brooklyn?"

"Yeah." I laughed, acknowledging how crazy the whole thing was getting. "Well, I needed him to get the drawings anyway. Mrs. Richardson asked to see them."

"I heard. That's wild. So how did the visit go?"

I shook my head, didn't look up.

"Not a lot in common?"

"I don't know what I was expecting," I said, "but my father seemed so . . . so uncomfortable. He really didn't want to be there."

"Can you blame him? I can't think of too many get-togethers more awkward than that. Maybe you need to give him some time with this. He must know your mom won't be thrilled about these little outings."

"Yes, I *can* blame him. Because it's all bullshit. All of it. They've got all these secrets. They all hold back the stuff they don't want to talk about and then pretend they're doing it to protect me."

"You mean Clover and your grandfather, too?"

"Even them, yes, but especially my parents. My father wouldn't say two words to me the whole ride home. Even after Mr. Mulvaney talked to him alone out in the hall."

"Weird," he said, sounding just as stumped as I was. Then he turned to me with this strange look. "I still find it hard to believe. I mean all that time Grandpa wasn't really your grandfather." He put his hand on my arm, maybe to console me.

"He *was* my grandfather," I said, pulling away from him.

"You know what I mean. He was never your mother's father— and you never even knew."

"That's not even the point anymore," I said. "They're still messing with my head. First Mr. Mulvaney says he mustn't see me again. Then he's calling to invite me to Brooklyn. Clover acts like he's the last of a long line of heroes. My mother says he's using me."

"What do *you* think?"

"I'm not sure." I wanted to tell him I thought Mr. Mulvaney was being straight with me, but I wasn't convinced that was true. My mom was unreasonable, stuck in the past, but the questions she raised were fair enough. How interested in me could he really be if he let sixteen years go by without making any effort to meet me? "He wasn't a very good father," I said. "Grandma had to leave him." It embarrassed me to say it. I looked down at the animal-shaped erasers in the box beside me.

"Maybe he had his good points."

"What do you mean?"

"I mean maybe he was a loser as a father but an all-right guy to know. I mean to have a few laughs with—as long as you didn't have to depend on him."

"That's not true. Clover depends on him."

"Okay. Okay. But even if you're right, your mom's never going to see his good side. She hates his guts. Maybe for good reason. She'd never want to admit she felt something for him even if she did." Something in Ansel's tone—an insinuation—made me uncomfortable. "Sometimes people have feelings they don't want to admit—even good feelings."

"I don't know what you mean," I told him.

"I think you do."

I wondered then if Ansel knew how I felt about him. The idea made my stomach get all funny. I forced myself to look into his eyes. "Are we still talking about my mother?"

"We're talking about pretending."

"My mom's good at that."

"That who you learned it from?"

"What is it you think I'm hiding?" I tried to sound as if he was being ridiculous.

Ansel let my question hang there, an excuse for his grin. "Oh, I don't know," he said, then leaned close and put his lips right next to my ear. "Maybe that you've got a thing for me?" The feel of his breath on my skin made me want to get up, but I tried to sit still.

"You're nuts, Ansel." I said, struggling to hide how embarrassed I was. "A thing for you?" I could feel my cheeks getting hot.

"Why is that so impossible?" He touched the inside of my wrist, making little circles with his thumb. It felt fabulous.

"I'm not your next groupie, Ansel." I pulled my arm away.

"Hey, I didn't say—"

"Ansel, let's get serious. I'm worried about these people. They're in some kind of trouble."

"Morgan, maybe this Brooklyn business isn't such a good idea."

"Why not?"

He hesitated. "I think you're running away from something."

"From what? That's ridiculous."

"From your parents, for one. Things are getting pretty warped there. And maybe from facing that your grandfather is gone."

"That's not true," I said. "I just want to help them." But I wasn't really sure what made me keep going back to Brooklyn.

"Morgan, they're not your family, no matter how much you want them to be."

I didn't understand why he was being so unkind. "I have a right to be with him. I have a right to know what's going on in his life," I said, getting to my feet. "If he's in trouble, I should be helping him.

"Maybe you're better off not knowing, especially about stuff that's over and done with."

I could see he thought I was obsessed with someone who was nothing to me. Mr. Mulvaney's problems were none of my business. "For heaven's sake, Ansel. My mother's been lying to me all my life. Why wouldn't I want to find out why he turned away from his own daughter?"

"Not to mention his grandchild. And you really think you can handle the truth about that?"

"I've tried to talk with him," I said, pacing now.

"Like the way you've tried to talk to me?"

I didn't know what to say. He was upset, maybe because I'd been avoiding him. "That's not fair. I—"

The heavy thump of Sarah's shoulder bag meeting the floor cut me off. "I've had it," Sarah announced. "If Arlene Peterson shows up to decorate tomorrow, I'm outta there." I was so relieved to see her. I tried to listen to them talk about Arlene, about the dance the next day, but my heart was racing.

"So she'll stay for a few minutes, then disappear when the work starts," Ansel said. "What's the big deal?" I stole a glance at Ansel. What was I going to do if he knew how I felt about him? How could we be friends anymore?

"If I have to hear about her father's campaign one more time, I'm going to barf." Sarah pulled up a crate and sat down.

"In another few weeks, he'll lose the election and it will all be over," said Ansel.

"What if he doesn't?"

"Then he'll be in Washington and maybe she'll visit him a lot," said Ansel.

I took a deep breath, still struggling to appear calm. "What costume is she wearing?" I said "Do you know?"

"She's not saying. Probably a Republican."

"If she needs horns, I've got some from last year," said Ansel.

Sarah looked up at me. "You in a hurry or something? Why don't you have a seat?" I returned to my spot between the boxes. "Did you make up your mind about Randy?" Sarah asked me impatiently. She wanted to know whether I'd decided to go to the Halloween dance with Randy McCormick. Sarah had been on a one-woman crusade to get me dates. It had started when I ended the thing with Hank the Hoopster, my chance at the big time—at least as Sarah saw it. Hank averaged fourteen points a game and was—in Sarah's opinion—more worthy of me than some of the other turkeys I'd been seen with. I tried to explain to her that the thing with Hank had consisted of one football game, one movie, and a hand up my sweater. I had a lot of feelings about not seeing him anymore. Grief was not one of them.

"I don't think so," I said.

"Why not? Randy's a nice guy," said Sarah, but I didn't answer. "So he talks a little. He likes conversation."

"McCormick doesn't make conversation," said Ansel. "He makes speeches. I think he expects people to kiss his ring when he's done."

"He's a little expressive," said Sarah, digging leisurely around in her shoulder bag for something. "It's part of his charm."

"I'll think about it, okay?" I said. But, of course, I wouldn't.

"Actually, you could do a lot worse than Randy," Ansel told me.

"She already has," said Sarah, working the emery board she had found in her bag.

"Save it," I said.

"How about that Cro-Magnon man of yours from Lawrence? A real orator," said Ansel. "Some of his grunts went to two syllables."

"Who? Max Campbell?" said Sarah. "I like him."

"He drools, for heaven's sake," said Ansel.

"And what's that I see down the front of your shirt when you're with Susan?" said Sarah.

"Will you two knock it off?" I said. "I'll have a much better time at the dance if I go by myself." I'd just about made up my mind not to go to the dance at all, although I hadn't told Sarah that. I didn't want to have to see Ansel with Susan, especially if he was going to be dancing with her.

"You can't go by yourself," Sarah said. "All the juniors bring dates to the Halloween dance."

"Actually, Sarah, I can." She saw that I was annoyed.

"Spoken with integrity," said Ansel. "A woman ready to risk ostracism rather than pair up with the likes of McCormick."

"Knock it off, Ansel," said Sarah. "And anyway," she pointed the emery board at him, "what ever happened with Ken Richmond? I thought you were going to talk to him?"

"Talk to Ken?" said Ansel, as if he had no clue what she was talking about.

"You mean about me?" I gasped.

"Don't play dumb, Ansel," said Sarah. "You were supposed to talk to him weeks ago. After he broke up with Louise."

I stood up. "Listen, will you two just butt out of my business?"

"Sorry," Ansel told Sarah. "Forgot."

"Forgot. Yeah. That's what you said when I asked you to talk to Steve Barnes. You promised you would, and you never did."

"Listen. If I want a date, I can get one myself." I picked up my pocketbook, slung it over my shoulder.

"I think Randy is your best bet," said Ansel, leaning back against a crate of Crayola crayons. "He'll take you back, I'm sure. He's so lovesick he's down to six meals a day."

I let him finish laughing before I answered. "As a matter of fact, I may give Max a call."

Ansel laughed again, but the laugh didn't match the look that came over his face.

I opened the door to leave. "Hold it," Sarah said nonchalantly. "I've got some news you might want to hear."

"I'm not interested." I figured it was another joker to consider for the dance.

"Yes, you are," she said with a grin.

Then I remembered. "About the drawings?"

"My mom wants to meet him."

"You mean she likes his stuff? Oh, my God," I said, pulling Sarah to her feet. She seemed just as excited as I was and gave me a hug. "This is so great. When does she want to meet him?"

"We'll have to figure that out," she said, lowering her voice. "This could get tricky."

I knew she meant my mother, but I wasn't going to worry about that now.

"I wish you'd come with me to Brooklyn," I said to Sarah. "It'll be so exciting to tell him about this." Already I imagined a steady stream of income from the drawings.

"Yeah, I want to meet this guy," Ansel said, closing the distance between us.

"You mean you'd come to Brooklyn with me?"

"Of course I would," he said softly. "We can bring your body guard here, if that makes you feel better."

"Count me out, thank you," said Sarah.

"Come on," said Ansel. "We'll do some research, talk to some of the homeless."

"Sounds like a great time," she said, then saw the look on my face. "Okay, when?" she sighed.

"How about tomorrow?" I said.

"I can't. Tomorrow I have to decorate."

"Arlene will take care of all that," said Ansel.

"Sarah, please," I said, and she didn't fight me.

"Okay, okay, already. Tomorrow," she said.

I gave her a hug.

"So what do they wear in Brooklyn anyway?"

sixteen

"Cauzzathepen."

"I'm sorry, sir. What did you say?" said Ansel, his face squished and wrinkled in puzzlement. Stooped over the old man on the ground, he gripped a pencil and a small notebook and tried to take down his words exactly. The gray-faced old man had chosen the narrow spot where a tie store met a card shop to spend his day. His huge raincoat encircled him, the pockets stuffed and bulging. His bright green stocking cap had "Jets" blazed across the front.

"Something about a pen," Sarah said, looking troubled. She didn't like bothering these people, didn't like the way they smelled. In fact, she had made it clear several times to both of us that she didn't like anything about Penn Station.

And even though this trip had been my idea, I didn't like it either. It was too close, too real. They did smell, and they did frighten me. It was like being in Brooklyn but worse. These people didn't blend in here. They didn't fade into the dreary, desperate background of a broken-down neighborhood. They were an awful contrast to the fancy storefronts and the busy, neatly dressed people hurrying by. It upset me to talk to them. They weren't statistics in a magazine article anymore or theories in a book. They had blue eyes and brown eyes and dark hair and gray hair. They were real. They were hungry.

"What does that have to do with his losing his job?" said Ansel.

"You were expecting this to make sense?" I said. I tried not to let on how uncomfortable I was getting.

Ansel took on each interview so matter-of-factly: the woman under the escalator, cursing, arranging all her bags again and again, as if their places in the beat-up cart made a difference to the day's prospects; the tall, ageless man with the hungry eyes, approaching the people waiting in line for New Jersey Transit train tickets to take them safely away to Bay Head, to Summit. The forlorn young girl with the dark hair, wearing old Nike sneakers. Her scarf looked just like one I had at home. You lost your apartment? Ansel asked each one. Yes. Where was your place? And they told him their stories, details about better times, about promotions and new homes. They seemed unpuzzled by his interest, as if they'd been waiting all along for him to come and ask. They'd had families, plans.

"We've got enough now," I said, motioning to Ansel's notebook. "Let's go to Clover's place." I didn't want to do this anymore. I kept wondering how long ago these people might have been just like me and my family, just like any other family. How long had it been since they sat around a dinner table or stepped outside to walk a dog? How much had it really taken for them to lose everything? It frightened me how easily it could happen.

"I'd rather go home," Sarah said.

"You promised," I said, reading the concern on her face. "The subway isn't that bad."

Ansel put his arm around Sarah's shoulder to give her courage. "Think of it as an adventure."

"I don't like it."

"A glimpse of the exotic."

"They dress funny here."

"Perfect. Think of all the fashion tips. It'll be better than Goodwill."

"I want a hot dog first."

"We're in New York City, Sarah. There are 2,657 varieties of restaurants to choose from."

"A hot dog."

"A true epicurean adventurer."

"Come on," I said. "We're bound to pass a stand on the way to the subway."

We got Sarah her hot dog, found the station, paid our fares, and waited for the D train. I felt worldly this time, an experienced guide for these two clueless suburbanites. We reached our stop, got up into the street. Ansel, for once, seemed to be at a loss for words. This was a far cry from Palmer Square. And Sarah was practically attached to my hip. She thought we should look for one of those yellow cabs. I told her we were only a few blocks from Clover's building, and that seemed to calm her down.

Clover answered the door, with Tina and John at her side. "Maud," she said. She seemed unhappy with me; she didn't smile. Maybe because she wasn't expecting me. I'd called, but I got some odd signal. She let us in. The place was cold and dark, lit only by the morning sun.

"Clover, these are my friends Ansel and Sarah. Guys, this is Clover Lynch."

"Delighted," she said, deadpan, and looked them over. She introduced Tina and John, but I didn't see Delores anywhere. "Come into the kitchen. There's tea," she said, apparently deciding they were harmless enough. The kettle was set on the round top of a kerosene heater. Clover avoided our eyes, as if we'd caught her at something. The flames of two fat round candles on the kitchen table danced with our shadows on the wall. The children had followed us into the kitchen, but Delores called them back to the other room.

"Is that Delores?" I said.

"It is."

"Clover, it's so cold in here. Why is it so cold?"

"We've no heat or lights." Clover answered sharply. "Since first thing yesterday morning. They were supposed to wait until November eighth, but they're ahead of themselves. Busy counting the dimes they'll save, no doubt." She saw the confusion on our faces but didn't explain, as if people like us could never understand that life's necessities weren't always assured.

"Why not?" said Ansel.

Clover looked at me. "He hasn't told you then?"

"Told me what?"

She hesitated, turned away, took more cups and saucers from a cabinet. "We've got none is all. Now, have a seat and we'll let the tea warm us."

"When are they going to fix it?" Sarah said, lowering herself onto the slippery vinyl seat of the chrome-legged chair. She looked mystified.

"They're not likely to be fixin' it." She set places at the table. This was what seemed to matter most to her, that we take our places at this table and talk, that we not let our routines be altered by those who had no heart, no mercy.

My stomach tightened and I noticed how thin Clover looked, how pale. This shouldn't have been happening to her. "They have to fix it," I said. "You can't live like this."

"Folks can live a lot worse. I needn't tell you that, with all the studying you've been doin' on the subject." The stuff in the books was nothing like this. They were filled with numbers, trends. The people had no names. Ansel and I exchanged a look, waited for the rest of the story.

"The building's condemned," said Clover, her voice stern. "At least it will be come November eighth."

"Condemned!" Sarah exclaimed. She stood up, as if fearing the roof might fall in on us right then and there.

"Rest yourself, child. It's nothing can hurt you. It's business. They're just going to knock it down, like all the others. Replace it with a building we can't afford." The words caught in Clover's throat, and I thought she might cry.

Sarah sat down, and Ansel and I joined her at the table. I was angry, although I didn't know who I was angry at. I only knew that people shouldn't be treated like this, like they'd lost their value and had to be dispensed with. "Well, they still have to give you heat," I said. "I mean they have to find you a place, don't they?"

"You'll not find me stepping foot in such a place as they'd send you to."

"Where will you live?" said Ansel. He looked worried.

"We're looking into a few things," she said. "I'll probably be with my sister Catharine 'til things get settled."

I heard the unhappy resignation in her voice. I noticed a child's cereal bowl in the drainer, a Mickey Mouse cup on the rack. "Do those children live in this building, too?" Sarah asked.

"Yes, but their mother hasn't even a heater."

"Jeez," Ansel said, seeing how serious this was. "What are you going to do?"

Clover saw his concern and seemed uncomfortable with it. "Of course, they're my real trouble, you see. There's any number of options I have for myself, but these poor souls—all they've got is me and Terence."

"No relatives?" I said, picturing them trying to go to sleep in an apartment with no heat, no way to cook.

"Still on the other side." She turned to the kettle and its weak whistle.

"Other side?"

"Puerto Rico."

As Clover brought the tea to the table, we sat huddled together, our coats still on. I thought of the people at Penn

Station and wondered if this was how it had started for them, too, this moment with no choices, no options. Clover saw me watching her and straightened. "And how are you doing?"

The question seemed absurd. All the little inconveniences came to mind; all the annoyances I spent so much time complaining about made me feel small and selfish. "Me? Fine. I'm fine."

"And your mother?" Her tone wasn't lost on me.

"The same," I said.

Clover nodded, understanding what I meant. She took her place at the table across from me in the shadows beyond the candlelight. "I take it your mother is still not interested in coming and talking with her father?" I didn't know what to say.

I glanced at Ansel. He was looking all around, at the heater, at the narrow window, at the fragile old woman. "But Mrs. Lynch, what are you going to do?" he said.

"Don't be worryin' yourself. There's a perfectly fine house for us, big enough for Delores and the kids and even Maud's grandfather if he isn't too stubborn to join us."

"Where is it?" said Ansel.

"Right here in Brooklyn."

"Well, then why don't you go there?" Ansel asked, but something told me it wasn't going to be that simple.

"Do you need someone to help you move your things?" said Sarah.

"There's some business needs tending to first."

"Clover, what are you saying?" I asked, impatient now.

"Never mind that. It will all work out."

Ansel looked at me. I couldn't help rolling my eyes. Another mystery. "What are you saying, Clover?" I said. I thought I heard the apartment door open, but Clover didn't seem to notice.

"The question is, have you talked to your mother?" she said.

"You mean about—"

"About talking to your grandfather."

"She won't see him." And the worried look on her face made it obvious that this had everything to do with their predicament.

"Do you think she'd talk to him on the phone?"

"She won't," I said, making it clear that there wasn't the slimmest chance. "Where is Mr. Mulvaney?" I said.

"He's spending some time at the warehouse."

"I'm going to see him," I said, getting up. "This is ridiculous."

"What do you mean?" said Sarah, beyond nervous now, frightened. "You can't leave us here."

"Sarah, calm down," said Ansel, but she had turned toward the doorway, looking as if she might let out a yelp.

"You wouldn't want to be left behind here, child, would you?" It was Mulvaney's voice behind me and it was gruff and angry.

"Mr. Mulvaney," I said. "What's happening here?"

"Nothing that's any of your concern," he said.

Clover stood up. "Terence, now don't be talkin' that way."

"She's no help to us. Her mother wants no part of us, and we don't need gawkers coming here."

I couldn't speak. I couldn't believe he was saying these things.

"Terence, stop that," said Clover. "These are Maud's friends, Sarah and Ansel."

"Sarah, is it?" he said and turned his great bulk toward her. "You must be the one whose mother goes searching for *artists*." He dragged the word out like he was talking about whores. "Well, you won't find what you want here. There's nothing to see, so get out. Get out all of you."

His voice was so loud the children came in from the other room. Tina pulled on his coat. "What's wrong, Mr. Mulvaney?"

He looked at the girl, then at me, frustrated and lost. He had no words anymore.

"Terence," said Clover, but he only turned and left. The door slammed hard behind him and the room got quiet.

"We'd better go," said Ansel. I turned to Clover, expecting her to explain something, tell me something. She didn't, but the way she set her shoulders, the way she turned to the window to look down into the street, made me suspect that she had made a decision, that something in her mind was settled.

seventeen

By the time it was over, two clowns and a box of crayons had to be taken to the hospital. Cleopatra, Scissorhands, and most of the other injured were treated in the nurse's office.

Up on the second floor, directly above the gym where the dance was held, Ansel and Sarah were waiting with me in the vice principal's office. Frankenstein was allowed to go home with his mother when she came for him, but Batman, Morticia, and me, Captain Hook, had been invited in for a talk with Vice Principal Krevitz.

I didn't know how the fight had got so big, but I knew how it got started. Everything had been relatively boring until I danced with Ansel. Frankenstein didn't like it much because I was his date. I never wanted to come as Frankenstein's date or as Captain Hook, but every other date Sarah suggested—and every other costume—seemed even more ridiculous. When I walked into the gym on Frankenstein's arm, Ansel recognized the monster right away: Max Campbell.

"I can't believe you came with that Paleolithic punk," Ansel hissed at me through his Batman mask. We'd chosen the south wall of the gym as a home base to watch the dance warm up.

"He's not a punk. Anyway, how did you know it was him?" I said, pulling my dark ringlets away from my face with my hook so I could sip my Coke.

"Yeah," said Sarah. "How could you tell?" In her spiked heels, she was nearly as tall as me. She made an impressive Morticia.

"The width of his neck, and the drool on the jacket."

"Better keep your eye on the Queen of the Nile, lover boy," Sarah told him. "She and that zombie seem to have an awful lot to say to each other." The warning was about Susan, who had come as Cleopatra.

I realized pretty early in the evening that it had been a bad idea for Max to come to the dance. The trouble between him and Ansel only put the match to the powder. Max was captain of the Lawrence High School football team, and Princeton High had lost again that afternoon to Lawrence. Some of the players at the dance were feeling pretty ornery about it. But Max didn't have the good sense to avoid the subject. Instead, he wandered from ghost to goblin, offering highlights of his plays, complete with sound effects.

Before the dance had even warmed up, it was obvious that something serious was cooking between Cleopatra and the zombie. But Ansel wasn't paying a lot of attention to it. He was too busy trying to keep Max from having a good time. Mostly he arranged to have his buddies cut in when Max and I were dancing—until they got tired of the whole business and told him to do it himself. So he did.

I had never danced that way with Ansel before. So close and slow. Frankenstein must have been watching the whole time, and he must have been watching when the song ended but our dancing didn't. Ansel held me even as the music picked up again, music that wasn't even meant for slow dancing. I didn't remember hearing any music. But I remembered Ansel's hands on my back and the warmth of his shoulder against my cheek. I never saw Frankenstein approaching because by then I'd sensed a change in Ansel's breathing, a nervousness, and I looked up at him to see his face. He looked back only long enough to pull away my beard, and I felt the cool air against my face and his warm breath on my skin. But in a few blurry seconds, I was on the floor. And so was Ansel. The rest seemed to happen in a single movement. Sarah was kneeling over me, helping me to my feet. Max and Ansel were on the floor just a little bit away, twisting and struggling, entwined in the Batman cape.

"Max, stop it," I screamed, but a pirate and a scarecrow from Princeton's defensive line were already putting a damper on Max's action. It would probably have ended there except Cleopatra pulled Batman's cape over his head as he tried to get up, tripping him back into a couple of clowns and giving Sarah the urge—which she did not resist—to pull the tiara off Cleopatra's head, wig and all. The Queen of the Nile squared off, but I shoved her off balance and the zombie pulled my coattails hard enough to put me on the gym floor again and that, as they say, did it. Ansel decked the zombie, then turned to deal with the zombie's buddy, a 200-pound scarecrow, climbing up his back. In seconds, the space between mid-court and backstop was a sea of swinging arms and soda spray, candy and broomsticks flying. The most serious injuries came when a sailing soda can met the side of a hobo's head and a broomstick got stopped by a nose. Mr. Conroy's piercing gym whistle brought more than half the menagerie to its senses; those who remained had to be untangled one by one.

Now that Mr. Krevitz, the disciplinarian, had pieced together most of the story, he was waiting to hear the rest from us. Sarah, Ansel, and I sat across the desk from him. He looked very unhappy. He had been at home on his big couch with a big bowl of popcorn, worshipping his big-screen TV with his big wife, when he was summoned to school. He looked at the three of us solemnly. He knew our names, our families. "Tell me," he said. "Do you think the thugs and half-wits that wear out my carpet every day here don't keep me busy enough?"

No one disagreed.

"Mr. Fagan, it says here you were hostile with a visiting student from Lawrence."

"He jumped me, sir," Ansel said.

"And you delivered several blows to the head and midsection?"

"I had to defend myself, sir."

"And so you enlisted the help of several gentlemen from the football team and then proceeded to do physical harm to one of our own students, too."

"No, that was me, sir," said Sarah.

"I."

"I, sir."

"Are you telling me it was you, Miss Richardson, who grabbed costume parts off one of our freshmen?"

"Just her wig," said Sarah. I tried to disguise my laugh as a cough.

"And Miss Lindstrum," said Mr. Krevitz, reaching down beside his chair for the battered cardboard replica of a knight's shield that had become the repository for a key element in my costume, "this, I presume, is your hook?"

I nodded.

"Mr. Krevitz . . . " said Ansel.

"Spare me," Mr. Krevitz said, holding up his hand. "I'll be brief." He fully intended to see the end of Showtime's *Creature Features* that night. "Upon leaving this office, you will join your fellow combatants in the gym and return it to its proper state—every last inch of it. Your parents will be informed of your antics." Mr. Krevitz paused. I heard Ansel breathe a sigh of relief, but I suspected Krevitz had more. He did. "And, of course, you will be suspended from school for the day on Monday. You'll receive a zero for all assignments scheduled for completion that day. The work may not be made up."

Mr. Krevitz was good at his job. He designed the punishment to fit not the crime but the culprit. Had we been the usual types—airheads and pranksters—he would have barred us from the next dance. But he knew nothing could be more upsetting to three little achievers than to jeopardize their chances for an A.

The gym looked a lot better now that we'd swept it, better than it did any day. Of course, we helped ourselves to the candy we found on the floor. Only fair. My dad was supposed to come pick me up, but I told him I'd go home with Ansel. Which was true, except I was sure my dad thought we were getting a ride. Really I wanted to walk home. I wanted to talk to Ansel about how to help Clover and Delores and Mr. Mulvaney. I had an idea, but I needed his help. Ansel said he had something to talk to me about as well. I wasn't in the mood for more of his apologies, but if that was the price of talking to him about helping them, I was ready to pay it. Anyway, it was time we cleared up this business between us. He was about to kiss me on that dance floor. And I wasn't the only one who thought so. I didn't know what was going on in his crazy head, but mine was a blur of confusion.

We left the gym and walked the wide hallway that led to the side exit. "So what's going on with you?" I said.

"I think we need to look everything over."

"What do you mean?"

"I mean take a careful inventory, as Mr. Kinsey would say."

"Last time I counted my fingers and toes, they were all there."

"Come on in here," he said, and pulled me into the auditorium.

There was no lighting except for the soft glow of the emergency fixtures set low along the aisles. Our steps echoed, and it was so quiet I could hear our breathing.

"So what is it we need to count?" I said.

"Tell you what. Why don't we finish our dance before we get out the calculator?"

I laughed. "We don't have any music."

"Don't you hear it?" he said. He took my hands and started humming the Black Keys's "Lonely Boy," the song the DJ had been playing when Frankenstein cut in.

I hummed along and Ansel pulled me close. It felt so good. He buried his face in my hair and said my name. I closed my eyes and kept humming. But then the humming stopped because he was kissing me. And this time he didn't seem the least bit sorry. He was holding me tight and his tongue tasted of the chocolate we'd been eating.

I kissed him back and there was no pulling away, no apologies. Before long his hands were exploring my back and making little forays around my waist and up my ribs. I didn't stop him, but then he moved his hand higher and he was holding my breast. When I pulled away from him, he had this huge grin on his face. "I knew it," he said. "I knew it."

"What?"

"You've never been with a guy."

I didn't correct him. I should have, but I didn't.

He took me by the hand and brought me closer to the stage, then lifted me up onto the edge. Jumping up next to me, he took my hands and brought me to my feet. Then, stepping away, he said in a booming stage voice—which no one was around to hear, thank God—"Ladies and gentlemen, students, young and old, it is my pleasure to introduce you to the sole remaining innocent sixteen-year-old in this pagan-filled high school. Indeed, perhaps in the whole state of New Jersey, perhaps on the entire East Coast."

"Ansel, stop," I said. I was laughing, but I was panicky because I wasn't the person he thought I was. I could never be that person. But he kept on.

"Be it known, far and wide, that it shall be my stated goal, my noble quest, in fact, to change that status. To persuade this young woman to give up her title. And under my careful tutelage—"

"Ansel, stop."

He could see I was upset. He lowered his arms and gave out a low laugh. "Aw, Morgan. I'm sorry. I'm sorry. I'll stop. I was just teasing."

He came closer and put his arms around me. "I'm sorry," he said, because by then I couldn't keep the tears in, couldn't bear the thought of what he'd think of me if he knew. Being known. That was really scary. Could someone know you like that—not just the honorable parts but the ugly ones—and not turn away? But once you opened yourself up, there was no going back. If they didn't like what they found, there you were, left alone, left wondering whether there was something wrong in the person you trusted or something wrong in you.

"Did I upset you?" he said.

"No," I lied. "I'm worried about them." He knew who I meant.

"Yeah. That's a pretty bad situation."

"I have to help them."

"You should talk to your mother."

"Oh, please. I've done that."

I wondered if I should at least try again to talk to my dad. But he hardly seemed eager to help. I knew what I had to do for them. What to do about Ansel I had no clue, but when he put his arm around me, I let him think we had nothing to worry about except grownups as loony as cartoon characters.

eighteen

Our house was so large that unless you listened carefully for Dad's study door closing or the slow churning of the heating system when it kicked on, like some long-suffering watchman on guard against the chill, you might miss the sounds altogether. So when I got up in the middle of the night unable to sleep and went down the long hall toward the stairs, I was surprised to see the light on in my parents' bedroom.

I'd had a bad dream, not a nightmare—no monsters, no tidal waves or hungry flames. Still, it sent chills down the backs of my legs and made my stomach loose and uneasy. In the dream, I was with strangers in a house so fragile it rattled and swayed in the shrill wind that came out of the darkness and ripped through the rooms. I woke up feeling weak and I couldn't get warm. Pulling the comforter up tight did no good. I fought the urge to run into my parents' bedroom. I could still remember when I would slip into the mysterious smells and secret sounds of their bed and tell them I was afraid and wanted to be held.

Outside my parents' room, I stopped, not sure what I wanted, but before I could decide whether to knock, the door opened. "Morgan," Dad said, surprised, "what are you doing up?" I saw the worry in his eyes and realized how awful I must have looked. I remembered the thoughts that chased me to sleep: Clover and Delores and the children in that cold, dark apartment, knowing they'd soon be without a place to live. And all the pointless secrets everyone kept. Were there even bigger secrets in this house? How much longer would my parents stay together?

"I had a bad dream," I said with a shrug.

"Not the crocodiles again?" he said, putting his arm around me. When I was eight and read *Peter Pan*, I had dreams about crocodiles off and on for months.

"No," I laughed, "no crocodiles."

"Do you want to tell me about it?" he said. He stepped back into the room and motioned me to join him.

I followed him in, sat down next to him on the bed, but it was as if I'd wandered in with no real purpose. "It was nothing," I said. "Where's Mom?"

"She's not home yet," he said, pulling a blanket over my shoulders. "You're still trembling, Morgan. Talk to me." I shrugged, but his words had loosened something and I was afraid I might cry. The shrug hadn't fooled him. He put his hand on my shoulder. "What is it? What's the matter? Is it the trouble at the dance?"

"How do you know about that?"

"Sarah's mother called." I slumped into the pillows and looked away. "I would have preferred to hear it from you."

"I'm sorry, Dad. It was late. You looked tired." He didn't debate this, just waited for the rest. "There's nothing to tell anyway," I said. "Mr. Krevitz got carried away with himself."

"Students were injured. That's hardly nothing. And for whatever reason, he believes you three were at the heart of it."

"It just seemed that way. It was Max. He went bonkers all of a sudden. Then the guys from the football team piled on."

"Why?"

"He was talking about the game all night. His fabulous plays. Lawrence beat us this afternoon. Max was gloating, at least that's the way it seemed. Anyway it was dumb for him to be talking about the game at all."

"I'm still confused. How did Max wind up starting the fight?"

"I don't know. We were all just dancing, and he came over like a maniac."

"Morgan, this isn't making any sense. There had to be a reason. Who were you dancing with?"

"Ansel," I answered, my voice small.

"Who?"

"Ansel."

"And Max didn't like that?"

"Ansel and I are friends. Everybody knows that."

"Everybody in your school knows that, but maybe Max doesn't understand how things are. After all, you were supposed to be his date."

"Does that mean I had to be on a leash?"

"Of course not, but some guys are like that," he said, sounding almost like a friend. "That type doesn't have girlfriends. They have hostages. I hope you're not planning to see Max again."

"I'm not going to, Dad. I didn't even want to—"

"Good." He put a hand through my hair. "He certainly wasn't worth a suspension," he said. "And you can't make up the day's work. Will that affect your grade in any of your subjects?"

"Not by much."

"Well, maybe the three of you can put the time to good use and work on your report."

"I don't care about the report."

Dad sighed. "Isn't it going to count for a fifth of your grade?"

"I'm sure we'll manage to get a B."

"That's hardly what they've come to expect from you, Morgan. Aside from the grade, it sends a certain message about your attitude. I hope you'll give it more thought."

"I have more important things to think about than a history report."

"What's wrong?"

For a crazy second, I imagined telling him what had happened with Ansel, how dishonest I felt about his thinking I was innocent, but he'd never understand. He knew nothing about what I'd done in Chicago. He'd have a stroke if he did. "I'm worried about Mr. Mulvaney and Clover," I said.

I could feel his body slump. We'd just entered the no-go zone.

"I think that situation is out of our hands, Morgan."

"What do you mean? They need help."

"What kind of help?"

"They're going to be evicted from their place. I thought Mr. Mulvaney told you about it, when he asked to speak to you out in the hall."

"He told me nothing of the kind. He just pressed me to speak with your mother, ask her to meet with him."

"And he wouldn't tell you what he wants from her?"

"No, and I didn't care to know, because I have no intention of approaching your mother about it."

"She'll only refuse."

"That's her call," he said.

"You don't think she'd listen to you?"

"I don't think she should talk to him."

"Why not?" I couldn't believe he was talking this way.

"Because he is what he is, and I doubt much has changed."

"You don't know anything about what he is."

"You may be right about that. One meeting is hardly enough to judge. But I know what he was, and it was bad enough to do a great deal of damage, damage that continues even now."

"What do you mean?"

He hesitated, seemed to be debating how to answer me. "Morgan, your mother has always had a great deal of difficulty trusting anyone. And now that Grandpa's gone she's curling in on herself. It's even worse."

"That's not Mr. Mulvaney's fault."

"He's a big part of why your mother behaves the way she does, and so I'm not terribly moved when I hear that a man like that is in difficulty."

"But doesn't he at least deserve to talk to her? He says it's very important."

"He's been doing this for years, ever since her brother Michael got sick. He thinks they can start all over again, as if they ever had any real connection." He stopped, looked away then back at me urgently. "Listen. Be careful with this fellow, Morgan. He's a user."

"You're wrong," I said. "They're in a desperate situation. They have no money, nowhere to turn."

"I'm afraid that's what happens to people who take no responsibility for themselves."

"They're not irresponsible, Dad. They're poor. They just need help. I'm sure that's why he wants to talk to her."

"How sure?"

"He won't tell me, but that has to be it."

"Morgan, there's a very good chance he's lying to you."

"Just because you and Mom lie to me doesn't mean everybody else does."

He looked startled. "That's not fair, Morgan. Your mother wanted to protect you. And even if they are in trouble, we don't need to get involved. There are dozens of programs for the poor. They can take their pick."

He sounded so hateful, so cold. I didn't want to hear anymore. "She wanted to protect *herself.*" I got up, headed for the door.

"Morgan, wait a minute."

"No, there's no point in talking to either of you," I said. And I had to make sure Mr. Mulvaney understood that, too.

I must have drifted back to sleep that night, but at dawn I was wide awake. I thought about walking over to Ansel's, but even churchgoers wouldn't be up at that hour and I was afraid I'd wake the whole house. That wouldn't be good. I didn't want his family asking questions. Of course, once they saw the car gone, they'd be asking plenty, but we'd be on our way by then. And if things went the way I wanted them to, we'd be back in Princeton with everyone in a matter of hours. Face to face with Clover and those children, there was no way my parents could say no. They'd have to help them.

I tried Ansel's phone, hoping it would be on. It was. He mumbled something into the phone, but I couldn't tell what it was.

"Ansel, it's me. I need you," I said.

"I knew it was only a matter of time," he said, his voice husky from sleep.

"Ansel, this is important. No joking."

"Not even one-liners?"

"Stop. Listen to me. We need to go to Brooklyn." I didn't hear a reply. "Did you hear me, Ansel? We have to go to Brooklyn."

"Morgan, I don't know about this."

"What do you mean you don't know?" I could sense where this was going.

"Mr. Mulvaney made it pretty clear yesterday what he thought about our showing up there again."

"Forget that. It's Clover and Delores we need to think about—and those kids. Anyway, he was mad at me, not you."

"Yeah? Well, he had me fooled."

"Ansel, listen. We have to get your father's car and go to Brooklyn."

"The car?" His voice rose, but he quickly lowered it again so his parents wouldn't hear. "Are you kidding? All I have is a permit. I can't drive to Brooklyn."

"We're going to need a car. They'll need to pack some things, especially for the kids."

"Morgan, what the hell are you talking about?"

"I'm bringing them here. All of them."

"Here? You mean to your house?"

"They're about to be put on the street and we've got a guest room here and Grandpa's room, not to mention the couches in the library and the den. The little girl could even sleep with me. And we could—"

"Are you out of your mind?"

"Have you got a better idea?"

"Morgan, this is crazy. You don't have to do that. All they have to do is go to the authorities. They can get help."

"You know as well as I do those programs don't have enough money to help everyone."

"That doesn't mean you have to turn your life upside down for these people."

It wasn't just the words he used. Something in his tone was so ugly I knew I needed to hang up before he said anymore. "*These people* are my grandfather, Ansel, and the people he loves." I didn't hold on for a response.

That's how I wound up grounded.

I got dressed, went over everything I needed to do. Then I waited in bed to see what my parents were up to. On Sundays, they never slept late, so I didn't have to wait long. I heard someone come out of my parents' room, then noises in the kitchen, so I went down. It was my mom. Bad news. My father had gotten up early and gone out—in his car. My mother looked upset, but I didn't bother asking about it. I wasn't interested in more lies, which was all I'd get. Without my father's car, I didn't know how I was going to get to Brooklyn. I was counting on taking it once he was safely spaced out in his study. Then my mother told me Liz was picking her up for another stupid meeting about the museum gala.

Perfect. I tried to call Clover, to tell her I was coming, but the phone was still disconnected. Just as well. She'd only want to know how I was getting there.

But I never got there. No sooner did I merge onto Route 1 than some road hog in a big-ass SUV pulled out in front of me and I sort of hit him. There was hardly any damage to either car, but the driver—a young guy with a big Alaskan malamute in the backseat—made a huge fuss once he saw I had no license. I apologized, told him I'd call my mom, then sat down on the curb and started crying. I couldn't help it. Everything was falling apart. The tears made the guy really uncomfortable. He kept running back to his SUV to get me napkins. Some of them looked used, but I didn't gripe.

Once Liz arrived in her Lexus with mom, the guy was ready to drop the whole thing. My mother told him she'd pay for any damages. That helped, of course. But Liz was doing a full-tilt drama queen, as if this fender bender could kick me off the society pages, and my mother was insisting we hurry this up because she was running late. Maybe he had a hunch that scratched paint on my mother's BMW was the least of my problems. In any case, the malamute was growling and barking, looking like he was ready to settle things his own way.

"What's gotten into you, Morgan?" Liz said. "I can't believe you'd do something like this." My mother shot her a look that short-circuited her curiosity.

When we got in the car, my mom handed me a tissue and told me not to plan on leaving the house again for a long while.

I asked if that meant I didn't have to go to school. She did not find that funny.

She didn't ask me where I'd been headed with the car until we got back to the house. "For a ride," I said, and went to my room to figure out another way to get to Brooklyn.

nineteen

The sun was setting and the house was quiet, as usual, so when the door chimes started sounding downstairs, they startled me. I tucked the little square photo of my mother and her family back under my pillow, the place where I kept it hidden. The photo never stayed there long; I was drawn to it, drawn to the faces that seemed so happy with each other, so eager to smile at the camera. I'd been cooped up all day and the night before. My mother had left for Hartford that morning, with strict orders that I was not to budge. She would have let me go to school, of course, but Monday was the day set for our suspension.

I wondered if it might be Ansel and Sarah at the door, but we hadn't made any plans to get together and they would never use the front entrance anyway; they always came around to the back. Louisa was already at the door when I got downstairs. "You can't be Margaret Mary," someone was saying to Louisa. I recognized the brogue.

"There's no Margaret Mary here," said Louisa. "Do you mean Margaret Lindstrum?" The old woman was nothing like any of my parents' usual visitors, and Louisa hesitated to invite her in. No one ever called my mother Margaret Mary.

"Lindstrum. Whatever. It's Terence Mulvaney's daughter I'm talking about."

"I'm afraid you have—"

I crossed the entrance hall quickly. I couldn't believe Clover had come all this way. "It's all right, Louisa. This is Clover. Clover Lynch."

Louisa looked confused but shrugged in resignation and stepped away from the door. "Should I call your father?"

"That's okay. I'll take care of it," I said, although I wasn't sure yet how I was going to do that. I didn't know what Clover had in mind, but I was sure she was here on a mission.

"Very well," said Louisa, and headed for the kitchen. Her final glance at Clover was nothing if not suspicious.

"Clover?" I said. It was more of a question than a greeting. I looked down at the bags at her feet.

"Would you mind if I rang the chimes again?" said Clover.

"The chimes?"

"Your doorbell. It's a grand sound."

"Oh, sure. Go ahead."

Clover stepped outside again and pressed her crooked finger against the bell. The chimes filled the large foyer, and Louisa appeared again in the entrance to the hall that led to the kitchen, puzzled and clearly annoyed. I glanced at her and shrugged, kept myself from giggling. Finally, Clover looked across the doorway at me, expecting something.

"Will you be invitin' me in then?"

"Oh, of course. Please," I said. "I'm just so surprised."

"It's a bit unexpected. I know. But at my age, it's best not to be puttin' things off." I offered help and reached for the bags. "You're a dear," Clover said. "If only I'd had you at Penn Station. But I thought as long as I was coming I'd bring a few things. You know. For you and your mother. We'll have no room for them where we're going." I wondered if she meant Michael's things, and the thought of my mother's reaction to them showed on my face. "I hope that'll be all right?" she said.

"Oh, yes. It was very thoughtful of you," I said, wondering what she expected to accomplish by bringing them. She clearly didn't want to face how hard my mother was about all this, how set she was against opening herself up to any of it.

"And a few things for my stay." Her stay? I put the bags down in a corner. "Why the place is like a cathedral," Clover said, and I realized that she'd been thinking the same thing I had. There was plenty of room for everyone to stay here. She looked up at the ceiling of the foyer, which extended up to the second floor. I watched her take in everything she passed as I showed her into the library, noticing again how agile she seemed.

"You can wait here," I said. "I'll go get my dad, tell him you're here."

"Jesus," she said, her gaze climbing the shelves all the way up to the ceiling, "sure it's big enough to be its own branch."

I smiled. "Make yourself comfortable."

I raced into the hall to my father's study, glad that my mother had left for Connecticut that morning. The door was closed. I listened. Black Sabbath. He was probably in the thick of measuring some black hole. I knocked. There was a pause, then, "Yes. Yes, come in." I opened the door a bit, put my head halfway through.

"Dad?"

"Yes." His head surfaced momentarily above the books and papers, then disappeared again.

"Dad?"

"Yes, Morgan. What is it?"

"I'm sorry to disturb you. I know you're working."

"That's not a problem, Morgan." But I could tell it was. "What is it?" he said, not yet looking at me.

"We have company."

"Well, why didn't you say so?"

"Unexpected company."

He got up. "Sometimes that's the best kind." He put an unlit cigarette—the nearest thing at hand—into his book to mark the page. "Come, let's—"

"Dad?"

"Yes, Morgan."

"I better tell you something."

"Tell me something?"

"I better tell you here, before we go into the library."

"Yes. It seems that way," he said, looking worried now. "Go ahead."

"It's Clover."

"What's over?"

"Clover."

"I'm not getting this," he said, and reached to turn off the music.

"The company. It's Clover."

"Ah," he said, and his body jerked as if I'd prodded him with something electric. "How did she get here?"

"The train, I guess."

"Remarkable," he whispered. "What does she want?"

That was the question, all right. But I'd let him figure it out for himself. "Just to visit. For a while."

"A while?" I saw it was beginning to get through to him.

"She's got bags. Two of them."

Dad put his hands through his hair. "At least your mother's not here." I couldn't disagree. "What should we do?" he said, but realized in the very next breath that he shouldn't be looking to me for the answers. "We'll have to tell your mother. That's all."

"Now?"

He smacked his pack of cigarettes to loosen one free then thought better of it. "No there's no need to do it now." He looked at his watch. "She'll be home by eight. We'll do it then. I'll do it," he said. He tossed his cigarettes onto the desk where the pack nestled between mounds of books, then he put on his jacket, donning a fragile composure. "Well, let's go to her."

He led the way to the library, like a dutiful soldier ready to face what he knew would surely defeat him, but Clover wasn't there. She'd found her way to the kitchen with Louisa, bags and all.

"The air will injure them," Clover was saying. "You should have them in water." Louisa looked annoyed. The disagreement seemed to be about the proper care of potatoes.

"Clover," my father said, offering his hand.

"Good to see you again, sir." She shook his hand. "And your mother?" she said to me.

"Mom is in Hartford. On business."

"And when will she be gettin' back?"

"Tonight."

"Tonight. Very good."

My father shot me an anxious look.

"Mr. Lindstrum, shall I serve coffee in the library?" Louisa said, eager, I suspected, for the chance to be rid of out visitor.

"Now there's a grand idea, but we should have some tea," Clover said and lugged her heavy bag onto a kitchen chair. "I've got it right here." Unzipping the side of the bag and reaching into a corner, she found the old mayonnaise jar and unwrapped it from a thick, hand-knit sweater, its protection on the journey. "The finest tea that ever steamed your nostrils." She handed the jar to my father and closed her bag. "But not in that canyon of a library. That's no place for tea. There's no better room for tea than a kitchen." Nobody contradicted her.

Louisa's shoulders slumped as she turned and put the kettle on, no doubt wondering if it was safe to put our the cream and sugar without getting instructions from Clover.

"The kitchen is fine with us," said Dad. "Isn't it, Morgan?"

"Of course."

"And your tea is truly excellent," he told her.

"You can stop that now, both of you. I know I'm bold as brass to be landin' on your doorstep like this." I couldn't help smiling at that. "I just thought we'd talk some," she said. "That's all. I won't burden you."

"You're no burden," I said.

Louisa took the jar Clover was holding out.

"And about what time did you say your mother will be back?"

"Eight o'clock, roughly," Dad said.

"Time enough. It's waited this long."

"Is there something I can help you with?" he said.

"Not likely," said Clover.

"You're welcome to stay, of course," I said, pretending I didn't see my father's look.

Clover looked pleased, relieved almost. "That's very kind of you," she said.

Before long, the tea was ready and Louisa served us at the kitchen table, but not before Clover told her to let it steep for what she deemed a suitable amount of time.

"This is straight from the other side. I have to go all the way up to the Bronx to get it. A little shop by Gaelic Park."

"It's delicious," my dad said.

"Is your mother a tea drinker?" Clover said to me.

Dad answered, "Mostly coffee now."

"I suppose it's for the best she wasn't here for my arrival."

Dad looked surprised by her frankness, but he didn't disagree. "I'm afraid you're right. It would have been rather awkward."

"Did you tell your mother that you came to visit Saturday?" Clover said to me. She didn't say it, but I was sure she was wondering if I'd told her about finding Delores and the children there and the apartment without heat or electricity.

"Not exactly," I said.

"What's this, Morgan?" Dad said, looking worried. "You went to Brooklyn again?"

"Yes."

"Morgan, you should—"

"Dad, not now."

"I think you should tell—"

"Dad, *shoulds* don't really make sense anymore, okay?"

"I don't think it's a good idea for you to be traveling to Brooklyn by yourself."

"Right, I might run into the big bad wolf."

"Morgan—"

"That already happened, remember?" I said.

Dad closed his eyes. "Morgan, this is leading to more trouble every day."

"What trouble?" said Clover.

Dad shot me a scolding glance.

"I tried to get to Brooklyn yesterday," I said.

"It's not the first time you've done that," Clover said, puzzled.

"In my mother's car."

"Driving your mother's car? Saints preserve us." She put her hand on her heart. My father looked down into his teacup. I stared at Clover's hands, the dark spots, the misshapen knuckles.

Dad slumped a bit in his chair, weary. He put his hand to his forehead, as if Clover and I were some mystery of the universe, and a solution was bound to elude him.

I glanced at Clover and smiled, because she was looking at me like I'd done something fine. Dad reached for the handle of the teapot. "I think I'm going to need another cup of this."

"Have all you like, darlin'," said Clover. "Why, there's at least a month's worth in that jar." As my father poured, he didn't see her wink at me.

"Shall we talk in the library?" Dad said to me, standing slowly to balance his tea.

"Okay," I said.

"Clover, please pardon us. I need a word with my daughter."

He opened the door to the library, motioning me inside with a gesture that seemed less patient than usual. Inside, he put his cup down, and we stood stiffly in the center of the room. I knew he wanted an explanation, but I didn't have one. I figured he could go ask my mother if wanted to know how things had gotten this far.

"Well," he said, "difficult as this is to say, it would be a mistake for Clover to be here when your mother gets back. I'm happy to drive her home."

"No." My defiance startled even me. "I'd like Clover to stay," I continued, managing a less-strident tone.

"Morgan," Dad said, "you know how your mother feels—"

"No, Dad, I don't." My voice was up again, thin and trembling. "Mom doesn't tell me what she feels."

"Still, it would be best if Clover is not here when your mother gets in."

"No," I said. "Keeping secrets isn't fair. It's cheating. And I'm not doing it."

"Morgan, what is going on here?"

"I told you. They've got no place to live."

"They haven't paid their rent?"

"It's not like that. And it's not just them. It's the whole building. And their friend has two little kids. The building is condemned."

"You're joking."

"They can't stay there anymore."

"You can't be serious." I understood the look on his face. It was just the way I felt, as if something like this just couldn't happen.

"They can't live there. It's going to be torn down. They need a place to stay."

He looked confused and concerned, and walked to the door. "Clover," he called into the hall. "Clover, can you come in here please?"

There was no answer.

"Clover, may I speak with you a moment?" he called again.

Clover appeared finally. "The place looks grand, Mr. Lindstrum. Just grand."

"Thank you."

"Why you could bed down a brigade in a place this size." I smiled, knowing exactly what she meant by that.

The two moved into the room, and my dad asked us both to sit down. I took the couch; Clover, the antique rocker that no one ever used. My dad remained standing.

"What's happened, Clover? Morgan tells me something has happened to your apartment building."

"We've lost our place, you see. They're saying it's not fit to live in," said Clover, keeping a tight grip on the arms of the rocker as it moved slightly back and forth. "Well, they can speak for the rest is what I say. My place is spotless. Always has been. Terence keeps the plumbing going. And you've seen his place for yourself." She stopped, seemed distracted, but then began again. "But they've given up on it. We've all got to get out."

"They've condemned it?"

"As of November eighth."

"But don't they have to find you a place?" I saw her face harden, as if this insult was one she was determined would not stand.

"Oh, they do, if that's the name you want to give it. A rat hole is what it is. I'll never set foot in it. You can be sure of that."

"Where is it?" he said.

"A welfare hotel. Can you believe it?"

"Can't they get you an apartment?"

"Sure. If you can wait two years on their list." She waved away the question he was about to ask her. "Anyway, I'm taken care of. It's Delores and the kids I'm worried about."

"They're her friends," I told him.

"Doesn't Delores have any relatives to go to? Friends?"

"Not unless you'd be includin' that vermin of a husband in the lot."

Dad looked at me. I shrugged, not knowing what she meant.

"Where is he?"

"Makes no bit of difference, that. He's a thug and a good-for-nothing."

"Well, he's got a family to take care of," said Dad matter-of-factly.

"That's an obligation he'd hardly toss and turn over. Anyway. She can't go back to him. I'm telling you. He was almost the death of her the last time she tried it."

"What do you mean?"

"He beats the livin' daylights out of the girl. Is that plain enough for you?"

Dad sat down on the step formed by the hearth, as if defeat had settled in.

"Don't be lookin' so discouraged, sir. The situation is simple enough to make right once some legal matters are addressed."

"You mean with the building's owner?"

"No, I mean with Mrs. Lindstrum."

"With Mrs. Lindstrum?" Dad got up. "Legal matters with Mrs. Lindstrum? I don't understand." Neither did I. And this time I was not going to be shut out.

"We need to straighten out some legal details, then everything will be right as rain."

"Right as rain?" my father said, baffled.

"As I said. And the sooner I talk with Mrs. Lindstrum, the better." Clover got up, and the rocker, moving empty in place, looked wrong without her. "I'll be no trouble to you in the meantime, Mr. Lindstrum," she said, moving toward the door. "I can promise you that."

My dad nodded, weary, and I moved to the doorway to call Louisa. When she came, I told her to show Clover to the guest room, that I'd be right up, but as I moved to follow, my father pulled my sleeve. "I don't believe we're finished," he said. He moved closer to the fire. "This is quite a situation," he said, but I could see he wasn't angry. "We'll have to get something arranged for them. He spoke as if he expected it would all be over in a day or so. My father believed there were systems in place for this sort of thing. Agencies. He put his hand to his forehead, wanting to rub some thought away. "Well, there's nothing we can do tonight. But in the morning—"

"In the morning? She just got here!"

"There are emergency services, I'm sure, that take care of people with these kinds of problems, Morgan."

"We can't send her away when they don't have a place."

"This is not for us to take care of."

"We've got to do something."

"Do what?"

"We have to let her stay here."

"Morgan, I don't think that's the best idea."

"Why?"

"This is our home . . . we can't just . . . "

"Why not?"

"Really, Morgan. I think it would be uncomfortable for everyone."

I felt my skin go hot, my nails digging into my palms. "Are we going to be more comfortable if she's on the street?"

"Morgan, I hardly think that would happen—"

"Yes, it could. It happens every day. I see these people every time I go to New York. They wind up on the street."

"Morgan—"

"And anyway, do you really think things could get any less comfortable around here?"

He looked at me, not sure where I was going with this.

"Go ahead. Look at me like you don't know what I'm talking about. That'll solve it, won't it?"

"Morgan, what is it you're trying to say?"

"Okay, I s-a-a-ay," I dragged the word out like a slingshot, then let go with the rest, "I'm uncomfortable that you and Mom can't spend ten minutes together anymore, and I'm uncomfortable that she goes out and never quite gets home at night, and I'm uncomfortable that this house is the last place either one of you wants to be—unless you're hiding in your study—so we might as well put the place to some use."

Dad couldn't manage an answer. The color had drained from his face. He made a gesture, reaching out for me, but his hand fell back to his side. "Morgan," he said.

He didn't know what to say, and it didn't matter because I didn't want to hear it. I turned away from him.

"Morgan, we should talk," he said.

"There's an idea."

twenty

Mom didn't sit down. She clasped her hands together in front of her like a prison guard waiting for an answer from unruly inmates who'd smuggled a buddy inside. "Can someone please tell me how this happened?" My father hadn't told her about Clover until she called from the office that night. He knew she'd blow. "I'm away for a matter of hours, and I return to chaos."

I hated when she talked to my father like that, like one of her underlings.

"We've got ourselves a situation, Maggie," he said. I could see he was not having an easy time of it. He moved to a chair by the chess set and sat down. Then he explained—his voice calm—how Ansel and Sarah and I had gone to Brooklyn and what we had found. He told her about Clover and Delores and what was happening to their building.

I was trembling. As matter-of-fact as he tried to make it seem, the events sounded shocking now. I watched my mother's face for a reaction; there was very little. She undid a button on her suit jacket, then another. Her questions were businesslike, focused. "Where is the father?"

"What father?" Dad said.

"Of this woman Delores's children—the one who's going to lose her apartment?"

Dad cleared his throat, as if not sure quite how to frame the answer. "He's not available at the moment."

"Not available? Well, maybe we can reach his press secretary and find out when his schedule frees up."

175

It was hard to listen to her, how callous she seemed about all of it, but I'd seen her like that before, when Grandpa was sick. I knew she was frightened.

"Apparently, he's not the sort you'd want around in any case." Dad picked up one of the marble pawns, stroked it absently, like a worry stone. "Rather incorrigible type, according to Clover."

"Ah yes, the gospel according to Clover," Mom said and glanced at me.

"He's a danger to the woman," Dad said, and gave her a look, as if speaking in code. Maybe there were just some things you didn't say out loud in this town. "I know Clover's being here is an untenable situation, Maggie, but—"

"What does she plan to do?" Mom said, not waiting for the rest. Dad didn't answer. Mom crossed the room to the desk, began sorting through the mail, as if this matter wasn't going to require much more of her attention, as if she already knew what she was going to do about it. But it wasn't going to be up to her, not this time. She was not going to treat me like I had no say. She just didn't know that yet. "Where is she planning to go?" she said.

"Social Services wants to send them to one of those welfare hotels," Dad said. "But that's unacceptable."

Mom waited for him to go on. He didn't. "To whom?" she said, tossing aside some junk mail.

"To all of us," I said. "Isn't it?" I stepped closer to Dad, stood by his chair.

"Listen, I can see you two have fallen for this," Mom said, "but we need to stop and sort out how much of this is actually true."

"We may not have time for much debating," Dad said.

"John, this could all be just another one of their tricks."

"Mom, I was in the apartment. They had no heat."

"That may be true, but that doesn't mean the building is condemned. They may not have paid the bill."

"I don't think so, Maggie; I think it's probably the truth."

"And what if it is? It has nothing to do with us."

"But Clover seems to think it does," Dad said. "In fact, that's the reason she came here, to talk with you about it." Mom did not seem surprised by this. "Some legal matters, she said." Mom gave him a dismissive look. "Maggie, I wish you'd—"

She raised her hand. "I hear you. I'm just suggesting we look at this carefully before we get too involved."

"We're already involved," I said.

"That's a mistake we can't change now." Her look showed no understanding, no tolerance of why I'd gone to Brooklyn to begin with.

"What do you mean?" I said, although I already knew.

"I think that woman made up her mind to bring herself here the day she met you, Morgan. And I think most of the rest is a fabrication."

"You think this was all some grand plan?" I said.

"I think you're mistaken," Dad said. "She seems to be in serious trouble."

"That's what they both want Morgan to think."

"Both?" I said.

"Can't you see how they set this up?"

"You mean Mr. Mulvaney?" I said.

"Yes. Your newfound, reformed grandfather. It has his fingerprints all over it. They failed with me. I wouldn't answer their letters. Now they're using you to get to me. There may be some legal matters to settle, but this is really about his wanting to see me. And that's not going to happen."

"Of course he needs to talk to you. They're desperate," I said. I'd seen from the beginning it was not about me. But that didn't mean it couldn't have become something else, something more. Still, it hurt to hear her say it, to be reminded that I was not really what was most important to them.

The look on my face gave my mother yet another reason to be upset. "Does he have you fooled into thinking he actually cares about you?" she said softly.

"Maggie, that's enough."

"Drink is all he cares about. That and getting himself out of whatever jam he's in this time. And he'll use anything and any-one to do it. He probably lost his job or drank their money away. He doesn't have the slightest interest in you."

"He doesn't drink anymore. Clover said so," I insisted, but my mother's certainty made me nervous. Maybe I was wrong.

"For now, at least, I think we have no choice but to believe her," Dad said.

"Fine," said Mom. "I'll look into this legal matter of hers."

Dad nodded and I was sure that he, too, suspected she might be right about them. My whole body felt heavy, slow. How much of what Mr. Mulvaney and Clover had said could I believe? They were in trouble, for sure. But why? Was it because he was drink-ing? He really hadn't told me much more about things than my mother had. They had never mentioned anything about the building being condemned until Saturday, when I went there with Ansel and Sarah. I thought of what he said to me the day I met him: "And if you knew what happened, do you think you'd know me better, the person here with you now?"

"I want you both to understand—and for Clover to under-stand—that I will not see him or talk to him or have any contact whatsoever," my mother said, looking directly at me. "I will not change my mind on this."

"No one's looking for anything you can't give." It was Clo-ver speaking, but her voice was so soft I didn't recognize it. I didn't even realize she was standing in the doorway until I heard her speak. She looked so small, so determined. Her eyes were on my mother, the look sharp and intense. Mom couldn't seem to take her in. She looked desperate, as if she wanted to hide, do anything but face this woman. For a second, I thought my mother might actually run from the room, but she just stood there, put her hands into the pockets of her suit jacket. Through the silk, I could see the shape of the fists she was making.

"Come in, Clover," my father said. "You said you wanted to talk to Mrs. Lindstrum."

Clover looked at him but didn't step into the room. My mother was looking at my father as if he'd done something shocking, but she stayed quiet, clearly struggling. My father gestured to Clover to come in, but still she didn't enter. "Clover, this is Morgan's mother, Maggie Lindstrum," he said finally, and Clover nodded and stepped inside, as if with this polite formality something wrong had been made right, and things could now begin. "Maggie, this is Clover Lynch." My mother said nothing. "Morgan, pull that chair over for Clover."

But Clover raised her hand and everyone froze. The swollen knuckles and crooked fingers were like a badge no one dared to disregard, all the authority she needed. "This won't take long," she said. She clasped her hands low in front of her, took a breath; the words came out softly. "I'm not welcome here. I know that. I didn't expect to be. But I have something needs saying."

"I think it's best if we talk privately," my mother said.

I didn't want that. This was my business, too. It wasn't her private affair. It never had been. I was about to say that when Clover spoke. She let a sharp breath out between her teeth and seemed exasperated, frustrated that her anger was already getting the better of her. "That's not what's best for anyone, least of all your daughter. We're best spared any more of your secrets."

"Clover—" my dad said, but Mom cut him off.

"That's fine. We'll talk right here," Mom said. Her face was flushed.

Clover straightened her sweater, as if to collect herself, and began again. "Your father received the letter from your lawyer, saying that you want no part of the property your brother left you." Mom began to say something, but Clover interrupted. "Be that as it may."

"Property?" my father said. "What property?"

Clover shook her head slowly. She seemed, like me, amazed at the extent of what my mother had kept hidden.

"My brother . . . Michael—" my mother began to explain, but her voice was barely audible, her chin trembling. We waited, but she couldn't go on.

"Shall I?" Clover said, and my mother nodded her head. "Michael Mulvaney, Margaret Mary's brother, left her some property in his will."

"What kind of property?"

"A house, his house. In Brooklyn."

"Maggie, what—"

I realized that had to be the house Clover had mentioned on Saturday.

"John, I don't own any house in Brooklyn," said my mother.

"You do now," said Clover. "Your brother Michael left it to you in his will."

"But why would he do that?" Dad said. "This makes no sense."

"His way of making things up to her, I suppose," said Clover. "Or more likely his way of stirring up trouble. We'll never know."

"Why didn't he leave the house to Mr. Mulvaney?" I said.

"My guess is he had some crazy plan for mending things between them. He was plenty hurt by Margaret Mary not wanting to see him, even when he was so sick. I think it was his way of forcing her hand, making her think about him finally, about him and her father. 'They'll have to straighten this one out together,' he said to me, one foot in the grave by then. He figured she and her father would have to talk finally. And, in the end, he was so sick he had no way of knowing what was happening to our building, what a fix he'd be leaving us all in."

"John, I don't *want* the house. I've already disclaimed the inheritance."

"Then what happens now?" I said. "Does it go back to Michael's children? Your father? What?"

"No, it becomes part of my estate," said my mother. "Apparently, that's the way the law works."

"And I'm here to ask for it back. On behalf of your father, I'm asking you to sell it to him. He'll pay—"

"Oh, stop it," my mother said. "I don't want his money and I don't want anybody's house."

"But Maggie, why didn't you return the property to begin with, get it out of the estate?"

"When Eric called me and told me I'd inherited the house, I told him I didn't want it. Period. I was in Dallas, the Exxon account. Our conversation lasted about two minutes. I didn't want anything to do with it. I told him to just take care of it. I assumed that it would be returned to them. Eric's office has been leaving messages for me to call him. I should have known there was more to it."

"How did you find out it wasn't returned to them?"

"She . . . wrote me letters." Mom said this as if the letters were blows she couldn't ward off. "Finally, I opened one of them. It said that the house was still not theirs. I've been meaning to take care of it. I just . . . I didn't know it was so urgent. I hadn't heard this story about the building."

"Story? You think we're lying to you?" Clover said.

Without saying a word, Mom looked at Clover in a way that made it obvious that was exactly what she thought.

"Whatever your terms are—" Clover said.

"Oh, please," Mom said. "These aren't the goddamned peace talks."

"Well, maybe they should be," said Clover. "It's been an awfully long war."

The room was thick with questions and confusion, but Mom didn't answer her. She was breathing deeply, trying to gain control. Her face was red and her fists were dug deep into her jacket pockets, pulling the soft material out of shape.

"Yes . . . well," she said to Dad, avoiding Clover's gaze. "I'll see Eric in the morning. He'll take care of it. He probably just needs my signature." She moved quickly to the door, taking the long way around the desk to avoid passing close to Clover. Before anyone could say anything else, she was out the door, striding fiercely, as if putting some insult behind her.

The stillness after she left was like a break in a terrible storm. Dad looked upset.

"You'd better go to her," Clover said to me.

"I don't think she—"

"Go to her, I said."

I stepped outside, but I didn't see her anywhere. The house was very quiet. Then I heard what sounded like a car door, and I ran to the garage.

Mom was sitting behind the wheel of the BMW, just sitting there, waiting for the garage's electric door to find its way to the top. She looked like she was waiting on a set for a director to tell her what to do next. Now turn the car on. Now drive out of the garage. Then go on with your life as if nothing has happened. I called to her, but she didn't look at me. I got into the passenger side.

"Morgan, I can't do this."

"I know."

"I can't be here for this. I can't do it." I didn't know what to say. She looked so desperate, so sad. I wanted to try to understand how she felt. Mr. Mulvaney seemed able to hurt her without even meaning to.

She looked down, talked to the dashboard. "I have to go into New York tomorrow afternoon. If she can't find another place by then, I may stay there."

"What do you mean?"

"On the West Side. At my friend Annie's apartment."

We said nothing for a minute, both of us trembling in the chill, stale air of the garage. "Are you sure this is about Clover?" I said. "You're so upset about her that you'd go away from me and Dad?"

"Don't make it sound so dramatic, Morgan. I'm away from you and Dad all the time."

"Right." The word came out like a little slap.

"And what does that mean?"

"That's what I'd like to know." I wanted to know why it was such a strain for her to be part of our lives anymore.

"What, Morgan? What would you like to know?" The question sounded like a dare.

"Why you have to be away from us so much?"

"You know what my job is like."

"Why does it have to be *that* job?"

"Morgan, a future takes money. Your education will be very expensive. These things don't just get handed to us." Her voice rose, but she caught herself.

"I don't think this is just about Clover. There's something wrong between you and Dad. Will you just for once tell me the truth?"

Mom rubbed her hands across her eyes. She looked tired, ready to surrender. She took a deep breath, but it seemed to give her no relief. She grasped the steering wheel with both hands, leaned back, as if needing to brace herself for what she was about to say. We listened to a car moving along the street. She stared straight ahead for what seemed like a very long time, and I wondered what other secrets she had, what else about her I'd never know. When she began, she didn't turn my way. "After Grandma left him, it took him nineteen years to get around to calling me. He heard you were born and wanted to see his grandchild."

"Really? He wanted to see me?" It made me want to smile. I couldn't help it.

"Yes. And I fell for it." Her voice sounded different, thin, almost like a child's. "He was in Derry. I sent him the airfare. Then I took you to him." She kept her gaze fixed on the windshield.

"What happened?"

"He wasn't there," she said, as if she were as baffled now as she had been then.

"What do you mean?"

She took a long breath. "We were supposed to meet under the big board at Penn Station in New York. That's where my train came in. I had you in a stroller. God, you were hardly two months old. I waited so long, just sat there watching for him. I was so certain he'd meant it, that he wanted to see you." Her voice trailed off. "And me," she whispered.

She sounded like a child, someone who had risked peeking out from her hiding place, only to find the world was still not safe. "He didn't come?"

My question stirred things up and she was herself again, angry. "He never showed. All he wanted was the airfare."

"Did you talk to him?"

"He talked. I didn't. He called me after that. He said he was sorry, of course. My father was always sorry. You could count on that."

"You didn't believe him?"

"All drunks are sorry, Morgan. It's beside the point." A speck on the dashboard caught her attention. She took a tissue from the compartment between our seats, rubbed it off.

"But after all those years. Didn't you want to talk to him?" I was amazed again at how easy it was for her to shut people out, no matter who they were or how important.

"I don't know," she said, setting the pack of tissues back in its place. "Maybe I just wanted to see him, to see if he'd changed."

"And he hadn't?"

"If he had really wanted to see you, he would have stayed sober long enough to do it," Mom snapped.

"Maybe something else happened that delayed him," I told her. "Did he say why he didn't get there?" She didn't answer. She held the steering wheel again, staring out at nothing. She seemed lost, as if she'd forgotten I was there.

"Mom, what did he say?"

"He said he was sorry. That's all he said. And something about never believing I'd actually come." She relaxed her grip, her hands sank to her lap.

"Oh, God," I sighed, feeling sorry for both of them. They were like two people who'd lost each other in a thick fog, neither one knowing the other was within reach. "But, Mom, maybe he really was sorry."

"There was already too much to be sorry for by then. I didn't need any more apologies. I needed him to make an effort, to show me something that could make me believe I mattered to him, that his own granddaughter mattered to him. He couldn't do that. So no, I didn't believe him." The rest came out softly. "Anyway he never got the chance to do that to me again."

She rested her head back on the headrest, weary. "So that's my reason, Morgan. That's why I refuse to talk about my father, or try to figure him out. I don't want any part of that kind of love."

I thought of Mr. Mulvaney's voice, of how kind he'd seemed. "Clover calls him a lost soul," I said.

"That's as good an explanation as any, I suppose."

"I'm glad you told me this," I said, and I was. "I want to know. I want to understand."

She shook her head. "I don't really understand it myself."

"When you talk to me, it feels better. It feels more like you really see me, like I'm a real person, not just someone you have to protect."

"Oh, Morgan," she said, "I've made such a mess of things with us."

"Just talk to me. That's all I want." She touched my shoulder. "Maybe Dad can take Clover back to her sister's place," I told her. "I'll find out what's going on." She didn't understand what I meant. "I mean about Clover and the building. I'll find out whether it's true."

"Don't be silly, Morgan. Your father and I will take care of this. That story about the building is nonsense. I'm sure Clover has bailed him out of some huge mess and now he's left her high and dry, without even a way to pay her rent."

I didn't argue with her. "I don't want you to leave," I said.

"I know you don't." She touched my hand, but she didn't promise she wouldn't.

"So you and Dad are okay?"

She closed her eyes, and I waited for her to tell me something, something to take the worried look from her face. But maybe, finally, she didn't want to lie.

Mom looked away from me, through the windshield, and it seemed that even in this stationary car, going nowhere, my mother had her sights on something far away. When I didn't say anything, she looked at me, and I could see that she was lost, that everything she'd been so certain about wasn't certain for her anymore.

twenty-one

Outside my front door, Ansel was leaning against the porch railing, arms crossed, hat on backward, a penitent look on his face. The night sky behind him was clear, the moon a giant circle only half colored in. I stood in my doorway, confused about why he was there. When I didn't greet him, Ansel let a few more silent seconds go by, and then said, "I'm just fine. How are you?"

"Ansel, what are you doing here?" He looked as confused at my question as I was at seeing him. But I couldn't get my bearings. I looked at my watch. It was past ten o'clock. "I mean . . . were we supposed to . . . ?"

"I'm just here. That's all." He looked sort of hurt.

"I'm sorry." I wasn't ready for this. Handling Ansel was hard at the best of times. Now, everything was a mess, and I wasn't in the mood to hear any more of his easy answers for the homeless. "Listen, I've got to go," I said, and began to close the door.

Ansel crossed the porch quickly and placed his hand on the door to keep it from closing. "Listen. I know I let you down yesterday. I'm sorry. But you've got to understand. My parents were really pissed off about the suspension. If they found out I took the car, they'd—"

I looked down at my sneakers. "Forget it," I said.

"Sarah said you're grounded. What happened?"

"I tried to go to Brooklyn."

"Aren't they getting used to that by now?"

"In my mother's car."

His eyes widened as big as an owl's. "Holy shit."

"I know. I know. It was a stupid idea."

"How far did you get?"

"Alexander Road. I hit a guy pulling out in front of me."

Ansel put his hand through his hair.

"But not hard," I said. He laughed, and it made me feel like smiling. "Clover's here."

"Clover's here?" His voice rose and I put a finger to my lips to quiet him. He came closer to me. "How did she—"

"By train. She just packed a bag and showed up at the front door."

"What about your mother?"

I had trouble swallowing. "It's bad."

"What a mess. What got into Clover to make her do something like that?"

"She said she had to talk to my mother." I closed the door behind me quietly, stepped out onto the porch, and told him about my mother and about the house in Brooklyn. "She's going to talk to our attorney tomorrow and get it all straightened out, make sure they get the house back."

"Clover's okay here in the meantime?"

"Not really," I said, swallowing hard. "My mother says she's going to stay with her friend in New York." The words hung there; we both knew this was bad.

"When did she decide that?"

I had trouble getting the words out. "She told me a little while ago."

"Kind of drastic, isn't it?"

"She says she can't handle being around Clover, being reminded of her father."

"Talk about holding a grudge. It's been decades already."

I shook my head. "I know, but I don't think that's the real reason."

"What is it then?"

I didn't answer.

"What?"

I stared into the night sky. "I think my parents are breaking up," I said, but my voice was barely audible. "I think she wants to leave, and this whole situation is giving her the right moment to do it."

Ansel looked worried. "Are you sure?"

I shrugged. "There isn't much you can be sure about around here." We were quiet for what seemed like a long while. "I better go in," I said. "Clover's still up."

"Let me come in with you."

Suddenly that sounded like such a good idea. I wanted to talk to him, ask him if he thought Mr. Mulvaney and Clover could have been lying about the eviction, using me the way my mother said they were. We went inside. We didn't see Clover anywhere, so we went upstairs to my room.

Ansel sat on the bed, stretched his legs. He'd been in that very spot a thousand times before, but it seemed different now. It made me nervous.

"I think your mom and dad will hang in there," he said. "You'll see. Lots of parents have rough times. They're good people."

"Good people get divorces all the time."

"I know," he said softly. He patted the bed beside him, wanting me to sit down. My throat felt tight, my skin hot. The air in the room seemed to be getting thinner. I sat down, close to the edge. "Hey. Why don't we go to the movies or something?" he said, and cuffed my shoulder, trying to bring me around. "How about tomorrow? We can see the one about the haunted mall."

"I'm grounded, remember? Anyway, I think Sarah saw that already."

"I mean you and me," he said, losing patience.

I looked at his face, still not understanding why he was acting like we could be a couple. "Ansel, we've known each other since freshman year. You've never been interested in me."

"I have so. We're friends."

"Exactly. But not that way."

Ansel held his hands out, palms up, a plea for fairness. "Hey, things change. I can't explain it myself. Maybe I like the idea of unspoiled goods."

I wondered how he'd feel if he knew just how spoiled I was. "We've never gone anywhere like that before, not just you and me."

"Why don't we do it and see if we like it? Something normal. I mean exploring the wilds of Brooklyn is all right, but sometimes I get a yen for the ordinary."

"I can't," I said. I didn't offer a reason and he seemed discouraged.

"Yes, you can."

"No," I said, my voice sharp. I saw what a mess I was in. Because I just didn't know how to tell him that the innocent girl he thought I was, the one who'd suddenly gotten his hormones jumping, was not who I was at all. If we actually started dating, I was going to have to be honest with him about the things I'd done in Chicago. I never thought I'd need to tell him any of that, because I never saw the remotest chance he'd be interested in me. Anyway, Ansel certainly didn't shy away from "experienced" girls, so what difference would it make? But now that he was making such a fuss about my being Snow White, I wasn't so sure. "I'm sorry. It's just not a good idea right now."

"Why are you being like this? Are you mad at me or something?" Ansel said. "Is it because I didn't drive you to Brooklyn?"

"I told you forget it."

"Then it must be what happened at the dance." He tried to pull me toward him, but I resisted. "The dancing," he said, his voice different, "it felt kind of weird, didn't it?" I didn't answer. "Good weird, I mean." He wanted a response, but I didn't say anything.

I looked at his face. He had this dreamy look in his eyes. It was pretty obvious what he was thinking about. I braced myself. "Ansel, you have this impression of me, and it's not exactly correct."

"I know what we should do," he said. He wasn't listening to a word I said.

"What?"

"Why don't we stop talking for a little while?" He pulled me down next to him and in a heartbeat we were nose to nose. I loved his face. It was so familiar, but up close like this it was so new. He pulled me closer and I could hear him make a noise in my ear, like humming. His arms around me felt so good, the closeness, everything. He kissed me and it was too hard to even think about stopping him. I kissed him back and his hand moved along my back, down my hip. "You like that," he said, because I let out a little sound. He moved his hand to my waist and kept moving up until he was near my breasts. When he touched them I was afraid to move. I didn't want him to stop. Before long he slid his hand behind my back and unhooked my bra. He found what he wanted then, stroking my nipple for what seemed like forever.

I moved my hand down to his jeans, slid it along his thigh. I let my hand brush against the bulge in his pants, hardly touching it, and he made a sound, like he was hungry. He took my hand in his and pressed it against the place where he wanted me to touch him. I could feel the shape of him. "Whew," he said, moving my hand away. "That's enough for the first lesson."

I knew what he meant. He thought I'd never done that before. In a way, he was right. I'd never kissed anyone like that before. I'd never been held in a way that made me feel like I mattered. What I'd done before was rushed and cold, and nothing about it had made me feel good. It was nothing like this. But I knew what he thought and I knew if I didn't tell him about Chicago, it would be the same as lying to him.

"Ansel, I need to tell you something."

"What? What's wrong?"

"I don't need lessons."

He answered me quickly. "You're right. I'm sure you'll figure it out in no time." He was afraid he'd said the wrong thing. He kissed me on the forehead. "In fact, I'm counting on it."

"This isn't the first time for me."

His face changed, and a few seconds went by. "Really?" he said, and I felt him move away from me, just the slightest bit, but he moved.

"What's that look about?"

"It's nothing," he said. "I'm just surprised. You know."

"Yeah, that's why I wanted to tell you."

"Well, okay," he said, but there was something wrong. He got up, so I did, too. "So I guess you'll be the one giving the lessons." There was an edge in his voice that I didn't like. "Are you seeing anyone now?"

"No, I didn't mean—"

"As long as it's not Max Campbell."

I realized he thought I'd been with boys since I moved to Princeton. "No, not Max, not anyone—"

"Hey, none of my business, right?" He looked at his watch. "Maybe I better get going."

In an instant, everything had changed. He assumed I'd been doing it with everyone. How could he think that? "Yeah," I told him. "You'd better go. I'll walk you downstairs." I didn't want any encounters with Clover to delay his leaving.

I opened the door, but he just stood there, looking dejected. I left the room. When I headed down the stairs, I heard his steps behind me. Halfway down, he said my name, so I stopped and turned. "Listen, Morgan. I was out of line just now."

"Forget it," I told him, because I didn't want to hear anymore from him. It was obvious he couldn't handle it. It had been a mistake to tell him. I hurried to the front door and opened it. He caught up and stepped outside, then stopped and looked at me. He looked afraid. I was, too, because something was slipping away, something so good.

"Can I ask you something?" he said, and I wondered if he was going to ask for a list of the guys I'd done.

"What?" I said, bracing myself.

"Did you feel it, too, just now?"

I took a breath, reached inside myself for whatever it would take to get control. I folded my arms in front of me and met his look. "Feel what?" He looked puzzled, and I was sure for a moment that I'd fooled him. I felt panicky, hoping he wouldn't fall for it.

"I don't believe you," he said, offering me a way out. He came closer, took my hand. I pulled away, and when I saw how hurt he was, I wanted to take it all back, tell him how lost I'd be without him. But I didn't. He stepped off the porch. I watched him walk away from the house, taking long strides, buttoning his jacket. I hoped maybe he'd turn and see me there, see that I hadn't gone inside.

"Ansel," I called, then again, louder, because I couldn't lose him, not now, not after wanting him for so long. He returned to the porch, waited to see what I'd say.

"I think you misunderstood me upstairs."

"I told you. I was out of line."

"No, no. I realize what it sounded like. But I meant that wasn't my first kiss. That's all I meant."

"Listen, it's fine. You're just fine with me," he said. But there was a look on his face that seemed a lot like relief. He held me then, and I buried my head in his coat. It felt so good, but it didn't feel right.

twenty-two

The notice was small, almost inconspicuous, posted on the narrow glass panel to the left of the door. Maybe that's why I hadn't noticed it before. I felt a rush of relief. My mother was wrong. The building had been condemned. That part was not a lie. If they were using me to get to my mother, at least they had good reason.

I stepped closer so I could read it. The building was to be evacuated November 8, just as Clover had said. That settled it. Delores and the kids were coming back to Princeton with me. I reached for the door handle and heard someone call to me. "Who you looking for?" someone said. It was a woman unloading groceries from a hatchback parked a couple of doors down. She was middle-aged, heavyset, wearing a bright orange parka, something meant to be worn on duty at some municipal job. She was not smiling; she seemed suspicious about what I was up to. "There ain't no one left in there," she said, standing arms akimbo with the weight of the grocery bags. "Who you looking for?"

"I'm looking for Delores Perez," I told her, but she didn't hear me.

"Who?"

"Delores Perez," I called. "She's got two kids, Tina and—"

"She left here yesterday."

"Left?"

"She left with her kids. She's gone. Nobody's in that building anymore. Everybody has to go. They're getting their things out. The building is closing on Friday. Everybody has to go."

"Yes, but she—"

"I'm telling you she's not in there." The woman seemed certain, but I couldn't help wondering if Mr. Mulvaney was inside. I turned to let myself in. "You shouldn't be going in there alone," she said, more urgently. I looked at her again, not sure yet what she meant. "It's a hangout now."

I stepped back from the door, noticed the beer bottles shoved into the corner of the stoop. I realized finally that the woman was trying to tell me it wasn't safe. "Thank you," I called to her, and headed back down the steps. The woman nodded and tended to her groceries again.

When I reached the sidewalk, I closed my coat. The day was getting cold and very windy. I wanted to try the warehouse, see if Mr. Mulvaney was there, but I couldn't remember exactly how to get there. Two women stood about half a block away, leaning over a stroller, shifting a toddler and some packages to make room for more. I headed toward them, and as one of the women looked up, the wind blew her hood away from her face. She was young, and I heard her laugh as I got closer.

"Excuse me," I said. "Is there a warehouse near here?" The young woman's smile faded and she and her companion exchanged a look. I didn't belong there. "You know, a place where they store construction materials?"

The older woman gestured before she spoke. "About three blocks that way. Then you make a left and a quick right," she said, as if eager to get me on my way.

"Oh, the construction company warehouse," said the younger woman, pulling her hood back up as the wind rose again. "Yeah. Three blocks. Then just make a left at that corner. It will be on your right. You can't miss it. There's a green sign says Superior Acoustics."

"Thanks," I said. "Thanks so much." I left the women, still negotiating space in the stroller, and found myself hurrying, though I wasn't sure what I'd say even if I found him there. I was relieved when I saw the sign. There was a doorbell and I pressed it, but it couldn't compete with the sound of a motor coming from inside. I peeked through the little window. Something moved. It was a kind of motor cart with a large flatbed attached. Mr. Mulvaney was driving it.

I banged on the door, but he still didn't hear me. I waited, and when the vehicle stopped and the motor softened, I rang the doorbell again. Mr. Mulvaney looked toward the sound but remained still, as if debating whether or not to answer. Then he saw me through the glass and climbed down. In a few steps, he had the door open. I thought I heard him sigh. "So," he said, in that way that made events seem so seamless, as if no time had passed since we were last together.

"So," I said, wanting to smile. I couldn't help it. It was so good to see him again.

"Get yourself inside. It's cold enough in here without that nasty wind."

Our steps on the cement floor echoed through the cavernous place as I followed him to the rear of the building, where a small door with a broken knob stood ajar. Mr. Mulvaney pushed against it gently and beckoned me inside. The room smelled like cigarette smoke and stale coffee and kerosene from the broken heater standing near the window. A metal desk took up most of the space in the room. A typist's chair—mended here and there with wide silver tape—faced a computer whose keyboard was so dirty the letters on the keys were barely discernable. Mr. Mulvaney cleared away some unruly stacks of paper from one side of the desk, then took a box of ceiling tiles off another chair so I could sit down. "I would offer you some tea," he said. "But the cups here aren't anything you'd want to put your mouth on."

"I didn't come for that," I said. The chair wobbled, so I shifted my weight to keep it steady.

"What did you come for?" he said. He stood in front of the window, his arms crossed in front of him, making the room seem even smaller and more unwelcoming.

I felt breathless and my words came in short little bursts that I couldn't control. "I want to know . . . my mother says . . . my mother says . . . you and Clover planned all this . . . "

"This is hardly what I had in mind for any of us." He mumbled his answer, as if he was talking not about us really but about the harsh, whimsical rules that govern how life moves along.

"Will you answer the question?" If he tried to bullshit me again and hide what was going on, I was going to leave.

"I haven't been asked a question."

"Is that what you were doing? Setting me up? So that you and Clover could get to my mother, put pressure on her?"

"They need a place," he said softly, without expression.

"My mother says that when she wouldn't answer Clover's letters, you tried to get to me instead."

"You came along when you did; that was all."

"So you were . . . you were pretending all along, about wanting to get to know me?"

"I was not pretending, not the way you think," he insisted. "It's true your mother didn't answer the letters. But then you came out of nowhere. We didn't know what to make of it. We thought at first that she'd sent you."

"But you knew she hadn't. I told Clover that the day I met you. I told her my mother didn't know." I turned in the chair and it tilted, so I stood up, but I still felt off balance.

"And what choice do you think we had?" He said this harshly.

"You could have been honest with me."

"Oh, is that so? You mean we could have sat you down and told you all about how your mother was ready to let people go homeless rather than give up her rights to the only home they had?"

"But that's not true. The lawyer couldn't reach her. She didn't know—"

"She doesn't want to know."

If he'd slapped me, it couldn't have hurt more. He reminded me of my mother at that moment, refusing to see things any other way.

"But what about me?" I said, flustered. "It wasn't right. You can't just . . . just go ahead and do . . . "

"You do what you have to do." He was staring out through the filmy windowpane.

"And use whoever you have to use?"

His arms fell to his sides and as he turned toward me, my breath caught. I didn't want him to come any closer. "What would you have me do with them? Let them sleep here?" He motioned to the corner. I saw the cot folded against the wall, a thin pillow tucked inside, and realized that this was where he was staying.

"You should have told me from the start. It wasn't right," I said.

"What's right and wrong isn't always just about you, young lady." He sounded almost like a real grandfather then, challenging me to look at something in a different way.

"What do you mean?"

"I mean they're going to wind up in some fleabag hotel or on the street. And I don't see much right about that."

"We could have worked something out." I wanted to tell him about my plan to bring everyone to my house.

"Your mother ignored our letters. You were our only sure way to get through to her."

"That's not fair, and you know it. My mother has good reason not to trust you. She has every right to be angry at you." The look on his face made me want to take the words back, but it was too late. He turned to the window again, stared at the branches going bare. The silence between us then was as cold as the room.

"I thought you wanted to get to know me," I said. "I thought we were friends."

"I don't know why you came here that day," he said, still watching the street. His shoulders slumped, as if his body was too heavy to hold up straight. "Maybe you were lookin' for some kind of hero, someone to tell you stories about fighting for what's right. Well, I'm no hero. There's nothing brave or fine about me. You know that much now anyway."

"Why do you say things like that? It isn't true. I know you're trying to help Clover and Delores. You're a good man."

"A good man does not abandon his children." His voice was tight, angry. "A good man does not beat his wife." He looked at me then, his eyes like coals that won't burn anymore. He saw the expression on my face, the shock. "So if you want a hero, you'd better look to yourself. And if you're so fired up about what's right and wrong, then maybe you ought to go find something—anything—in this godforsaken world that you can change for the better."

He strode past me to the door, letting in the cold air of the warehouse as he moved outside. I sat back down for what seemed like a long time, absently tracing the coffee rings on the desk, imagining how he'd treated my grandmother. He was being direct with me, honest. But his truth was too hard. It frightened me.

I got up, blinked against the sunlight reflecting off a passing bus. In the warehouse, Mr. Mulvaney was about to climb back onto his cart. "Clover can stay with us," I told him. "Don't worry about her."

I walked toward the door without saying any more, but he called to me. "Wait," he said. "I'm working on something with a cousin of mine. A place for them. But it's going to take a day or two. Just so's you know."

I nodded. "She can stay as long as it takes. So can Delores and the kids. If my parents put them out, you'll have to find a place for me, too."

He nodded. "You're a good girl, Maud," he said. "But they're safe where they are 'til Friday. The apartment's good 'til then."

"They're not at the apartment. I was just there."

"What do you mean not there?"

"A woman outside the building told me there are no tenants in there anymore."

"She don't know what she's talking about," he said, but he looked worried.

"Do you want me to go check? I can stop by again on my way back."

"No," he said, almost harshly. "I'm leaving as soon as that delivery gets here. Wait here and we'll go together."

"I can't," I said. "I have to get back." I'd cut two classes to get here. The school had probably called my mother by now, probably my father, too, although neither one had called my cell yet. I moved toward the door, but he stopped me again.

"Maud," he said, "that stuff you said—about pretending. I wasn't pretending. Not about you and me." I wasn't sure what to say, or even whether I believed him. "I just knew that sooner or later you'd find out—about the kind of man I was, and about how I never took the trouble to see my own grandchild—and that would be the end of it. You'd want no part of me."

His voice carried harshly through the warehouse, louder than intended. And I had no answer for him, because maybe he wasn't so wrong about that.

twenty-three

Ansel and Sarah didn't realize I'd come into the dining room. They were too busy listening to Clover telling them about Catholics in Northern Ireland, about how poor they were. The table was stacked high with books. Index cards were spread all over—color-coded with thick round dots of blue, green, and red in each corner. As soon as Ansel saw me, he stood up and came over. "Where've you been? You disappeared after fifth period," he said, but only loud enough for me to hear.

I knew they'd be wondering what was going on when I walked out of school like that. But I wasn't ready to talk about where I'd been or what Mr. Mulvaney had said, the way he had treated my grandmother, not now, not with Sarah here.

"Morgan, you can't just take off—"

"Sarah, please," I said. "Not now, okay?"

Sarah got quiet and Ansel sat down. Nobody knew what to say. We dutifully took our places, looked down at the work we had to do. Ansel reached for a book; Sarah did the same.

"We've got a lot of ground to cover," said Sarah.

"Well, it can wait one more moment," said Clover. Ansel and I exchanged a look. "First, young lady, you can tell us where you've been all afternoon."

"She wasn't in school this afternoon," Sarah chimed in, clearly glad we were back on the subject. "We looked all over for her."

"We can talk about it later," I said.

"We can talk about it now," said Clover. "Where did you take yourself off to?" Her tone wasn't harsh, but I could see that she was not going to let go of this.

"I went to Brooklyn."

"You needed to see things for yourself then?" she said. It was a question she didn't need me to answer. So I didn't. I didn't even nod my head. I was ashamed that I had thought she might not be telling the truth. "Well, that's settled, anyway," she said, but I could hear the hurt in her voice. "Did you talk to Delores?"

"No," I said. "I talked to Mr. Mulvaney."

"That's odd," she said. "He's supposed to be at the warehouse. There's a big delivery this afternoon."

"He *was* at the warehouse. That's where I talked to him."

"Then who was at the apartment?" she said, clearly puzzled now.

"I'm not really sure," I said. "A woman from next door said no one was in the building anymore. She said everyone had moved their stuff out, moved on."

"She's mistaken. My things are still there. I left Delores there with the children. We don't have to be out 'til Monday—November eighth."

"That's what Mr. Mulvaney said. But I stopped at the grocery store on the way back from the warehouse, the one where she works. The man said he hasn't seen Delores since yesterday. He wasn't pleased about it, said she didn't come into work today."

"That can't be right," Clover said. She seemed angry with me.

"I'm sorry," I said, feeling suddenly responsible for something terrible. "I thought maybe one of the kids was sick, so she didn't go to work. I don't understand. What's wrong?"

But she didn't answer. Her hands came together nervously.

"I'm sorry. I should have gone up to see for myself, but the woman said it was dangerous to go in, so I . . . "

Clover lifted a hand to silence me. "When I left, I told her I wouldn't give up 'til I'd spoken to your mother. She must have thought I wouldn't return. She's gone back to him."

"Back to who? What are you talking about?" Ansel said.

"She's gone back to her husband."

"But she can't go there," I said. I couldn't believe Delores would do that. Not after what Clover had said about him.

"It's done, child."

"She wouldn't do that. He beats her. Isn't that what you said? That he beats her?"

"She'd do it if she thought there was no other way."

"What do you mean no other way?" My voice was loud now. "Didn't you tell her you were coming here? That you'd talk to my mother?"

"Of course I told her. She saw no point in it. She didn't think your mother would even see me."

"Where is this guy?" said Ansel.

"Brooklyn."

"Can't we call her there," I said, "let her know everything's going to be all right?"

"There's no phone in the apartment."

"Call her cell," said Sarah, and Clover almost smiled at her.

"She has no cell."

"We'll have to go there then," I said.

"He's a dangerous man, Maud. This is not for you to be handlin'."

"We have to do something." If we waited for my parents to do something, who knew how much worse things would get?

I looked at Ansel, and he understood what I wanted him to do. "Do you know where the place is?" he said to Clover.

"I do."

"Where's my father?" I said.

"He went out a little while ago," said Sarah.

205

"He wants to see what he can find out about the building's owners," said Clover. "He's wasting his time. I told him that."

"Ansel, we'll have to use your mom's car to get there."

"Get where?" said Sarah.

"To Brooklyn," said Ansel.

Clover raised her eyes heavenward, made the sign of the cross, saying, "The lord protect us."

"Amen to that," said Sarah. "But I'm wearing a seatbelt."

twenty-four

Ansel didn't like driving to Brooklyn. When he sneaked out in his parents' Mercedes for a drive with Sarah and me, he'd stick to quiet country lanes and wide county roads, maybe an occasional highway when it was dark. His brow was sweaty for the whole ride, and I wanted to put my hand on his arm to show him how proud I was, but I settled for telling him he was doing a great job. "Then why are all these horns blaring at me?" he said.

"Because they recognize you," said Sarah. "High school basketball is big around here."

Ansel smiled and Clover told him not to worry. We were almost there and the car was still in one piece. "No one's going to count the scrape on the side door," she assured him. "It wasn't your fault. That van was parked like a getaway car."

Ansel couldn't find a parking spot on 48th Street big enough for him to manage, so he pulled up behind a garbage dumpster in a no-parking zone.

"All right then," said Clover as Ansel turned the car off. "You stay here."

"Forget it," I told her. "I'm going with you."

"You two are going to be in enough trouble," she said. "I'll take care of this. Just mind the car."

"I didn't risk my license to sit here like a flunky," said Ansel. "What floor is she on?"

"Third," said Clover.

I let myself out of the Mercedes, and the suddenness of the street noise was like an assault.

Ansel opened the door for Clover, and she took the lead, her steps firm, her long woolen coat flapping. We followed her to the other side of the street, stepped carefully between the parked cars and into the dismal building. The condition of the place was hardly any better than Clover's. We reached the apartment door and listened. There was no sound of children. Nothing. And I wondered for a second whether they'd left already, found somewhere else to go. Clover knocked, but it remained quiet. "Do you think she's gone?" I said.

"No, darlin'," Clover explained, and I realized how much I wished she were. "She must think we're bill collectors. We've got to call her name." Ansel nodded, as if Clover should proceed. "Delores," she called. "Delores."

We heard something from inside, a few high-pitched syllables. Maybe John. Then footsteps. The door opened as far as the chain lock would let it, revealing only one suspicious eye. Delores looked at us and shook her head. "You must go away," she said.

"Let us talk to you, Delores," said Clover. "We've got grand news."

"No. You must go."

"*Quién es ese?*" A man's voice called from a room far into the apartment. Delores answered him hurriedly, an attempt to soothe. Then she turned to Clover again. "You have to go."

"We just want to talk," Clover began, but the man spoke again, louder, more menacing this time.

"Please go," Delores whispered.

"We're not going," I said. "Not without you and the kids."

Clover put a hand on my arm, a caution not to rush this. "We can't leave her here. He's going to hurt them," I said, and stepped in front of Clover. "Listen to me, Delores. We brought a car. We can fit all your things. And Ansel's a really good driver." I hoped she couldn't hear Sarah snickering. "Please let us in."

"No one ask you to come here," Delores said.

"I know you're upset," Clover said, her voice calmer than mine. "But you can't stay here, darlin'. This is not the answer."

"I find my own answers."

"Delores, I talked to Margaret Mary," said Clover. "We can have Michael's house. It's just a matter of getting things straightened out."

Delores listened, her expression softening, as if flirting with hope. "I've lost my job for sure," she whispered.

"We'll explain things to Hector. He'll listen," said Clover. "You're the best worker he's ever had. He knows that."

Delores looked at her. "Let us in, darlin'," Clover said.

The door closed then opened again wide, and we could see all of Delores's face clearly now. It was bruised, one eye swollen. I heard Sarah's sharp intake of breath at the sight of it.

"Where are the children?" I said. I moved past Delores and headed quickly down the long hall.

"In the bedroom."

"Please get them," I said. I was way ahead of the others now, and Delores was calling my name, trying to catch up, obviously afraid for me. But I kept moving. All my anger had found a worthy target. I liked it. I felt reckless, but I couldn't stop.

The children came out of the room at the end of the hall just as I reached the entrance to the living room. Delores caught up to me first. Tina's face, too, was bruised. She stood frozen in place, but John began crying and headed straight for Clover, burying his face in the old woman's coat. I saw that this was a man who should not be bargained with. Their fear of him had become part of who they were, part of the way they held their bodies. It reminded me of my grandmother, how she had received the smallest kindness as if it would eventually have a price.

In the living room, a slim, dark-haired man in a sweatshirt and jeans was sitting on the couch, the television blasting. "Sarah, find their coats," I said. My voice was hard.

The man got to his feet. "Who are you?"

"Maud Lindstrum. Pleased to meet you," I said, deadpan, then told Clover to help Delores gather their things.

The man didn't need to ask what we wanted. My directions made that clear enough. "Get out," the man barked.

The yelling scared me, but I let him think it made no impression. "We'll only be a moment, sir," I told him.

"You get out," he yelled, pointing his finger at me, threatening. Tina began to cry again, knowing what might come. The man looked like a wiry coil about to spring.

"Carlos, *por favor* . . ." Delores said.

John began crying even louder as Delores pleaded with her husband. Lady Gaga was screaming from the television screen, and Clover was calling on saints. Sarah was squeaking like a mouse backing into its hole. Everyone was afraid, and so was I. It was all I could do not to run back out the door. But I was determined not to let this man see how frightened I was. I turned to face him; I was taller than he was, and I certainly appeared calmer. "We'll only be a moment, Carlos," I said to him. I turned away before he could start shouting again and I pointed to something in the corner. "That bear. Does John sleep with that? We'll need that," I said to no one in particular and started toward it. But the man leaped at me, pushed me off balance, and I fell onto the couch, stunned.

My fear brought something else with it this time—I wanted to hurt him. I got back on my feet, lunged at him, heard Clover call on still more saints, heard Delores and the children crying, felt the man grab my arms. I pushed at him, frustrated at his strength. I slipped an arm free, but found all at once that there was no one to hit. Ansel had knocked him to the floor, where he lay in a tangle with Delores and the children. I bent to help them, but Ansel had me by the waist, pulling me away. We both fell, and in the second or two it took for me to get my bearings,

I saw the man rise above us, as if he'd been picked like a kitten from a litter, moving into the air, his legs dangling, his lean arms flailed uselessly, unable to connect, as Mr. Mulvaney held him by the back of his shirt, the way a tired old lioness might chastise an unruly cub.

"Are you hurt, Morgan?" Ansel said, breathless.

"No, I'm okay." He pulled me to him again, relieved, then got to his feet and reached down to help me up. Sarah peeked out from behind an armchair.

"Be still," Mr. Mulvaney told Carlos, but the man continued to flail. "Be still," he scolded, "or I'll have to slug you." But Carlos wouldn't stop swinging, so he did. The stricken man was so surprised his eyes crossed, his mouth fell slack-jawed.

"Where shall I put him?" Mr. Mulvaney said to Clover.

"Why don't you two just rest yourselves on the couch while Delores gets her things together?"

Mr. Mulvaney put Carlos on the couch and took the spot beside him. The smaller man leaned on the older one, and except for the trickle of blood near his nose, he looked no worse than if he'd had a bit too much to drink.

Delores ran to the kitchen and returned with a towel to wash the blood away from her husband's nose. She reached tentatively to wipe his face. "Here," said Mr. Mulvaney. "I'll do that. You get packed up." Delores went back to gathering her things, holding John with one arm and picking up toys with the other. She kept one eye on her husband. Mr. Mulvaney dabbed ungently at Carlos's nose, but he was too woozy to protest.

"Well, Terence," said Clover, "we're glad you decided to drop by." Ansel was the first to break up, then me, until all of us were laughing—even Delores. Mr. Mulvaney only grinned. His companion sat dazed and unsmiling, like a drunken soccer fan beginning to suspect he's on the wrong side of the stadium.

twenty-five

I was the first one downstairs, carrying John's Teddy bear and some other toys. Ansel and I helped Delores load her things into the trunk. There wasn't much: two suitcases, a box of toys. Everything fit except a plastic shopping bag that belonged to Tina. She wouldn't part with it, so they made room for it on the floor in the back.

We stood near the car when we were done. John had climbed into the back and was making a game of sliding off the leather seat. Clearly uncomfortable, Mr. Mulvaney shifted his weight nervously from one leg to the other. He wouldn't look at me. Clover was talking nonstop, going on about the expression on Carlos's face as he watched us gather the children's things. I heard only parts of what she said because there was so much going on in my head. Mr. Mulvaney had come here for no other reason than to help Delores. He knew exactly what kind of danger she was in. My mother was wrong about her father. She had to be. He just wasn't that person anymore.

"How did you know to come here?" Clover said.

Mr. Mulvaney explained that he had gone back to the apartment building to check on Delores once the delivery arrived at the warehouse. When he talked with Hector at the store, he realized that Delores must have gotten desperate enough to go back to her husband. That's when he headed for Carlos's place. Clover described the ride to Brooklyn, how Delores didn't want to let us in.

I wanted to say something to Mr. Mulvaney, but I didn't know what it should be. Clover finally got quiet, and we stood there as if encased in glass. The wind picked up, lifting my hair across my face. I saw him look at me. I couldn't read his expression, but his eyes were watery.

"Is Mr. Mulvaney coming to Princeton with us, too?" said Tina.

The question made Mr. Mulvaney cough and startled Delores into saying something I couldn't catch, but Clover answered the girl. "No, Tina."

"Well," said Mr. Mulvaney. "I'd best be goin'." He leaned and kissed Clover on the cheek. "We'll have news soon, I hope," I heard him tell her. He looked down the street, hesitant, like someone uncertain whether or not he had missed his bus. He was stone-faced, his mouth tightly closed, holding back something so big it would surely come out on its own if he wasn't careful. "Good to see you again," he said finally—ridiculously—tipping his cap to me, the way he probably did to the mailman or to any acquaintance he'd see every day. "Very good," he said and waited a beat, as if maybe this time I'd answer. But I didn't, and he headed away.

I watched him leave us, wondering if I'd ever see him again. I didn't know what to do, but I knew this wasn't right, to let him go without saying something. "Mr. Mulvaney," I called. "Mr. Mulvaney." In a few strides, I caught up to him. "I just want to say, well, I just want to tell you how glad I am that you got here."

He looked at me and a smile played at the corners of his mouth, as if what he saw in my face was enough for him. "That's very nice to hear, but it looked to me as if you were handling things just fine."

"I'm not so sure about that," I laughed.

He leaned toward me. "I'm very proud of you, Maud," he said, close to my ear.

"Mr. Mulvaney," I said, but my voice was breaking. "We ought to have hot chocolate again . . . or . . . or something."

He sighed and touched my shoulder. "Yes," he said, like he was trying to figure out the right thing to do, but instead he just removed his cap and stood there, waiting for something, wishing for it. But for what? The right words, permission to say them, for the past to finally be over, for this moment, here with me, to be the one that really counted? I wanted the same things. But he put his cap back on, and I saw that he was about to move on—and that I was too afraid to stop him.

We looked toward the car. Ansel and the others were looking our way, waiting for me, waiting to see what I would do. "I'm not looking forward to the drive back," I said. "Ansel doesn't exactly have much experience at the wheel."

"He does look a bit wet behind the ears. How long has he had his license?"

"He doesn't exactly have one."

"What? No license? Jesus, Mary, and Joseph." He looked at Ansel, then back at me, ready to blow, just as I expected. "You can't be doing this, Maud. You can't have him behind the wheel with those kids in the car, with all of you in the car."

"But I can't drive either, not on highways like the ones we have to use."

"I'll drive you home," he said, already moving toward the car.

"But you don't have a license," I said, catching up. "Clover said so."

"Then I'll have nothing to lose if they stop me then, will I? Let's go." And he led me back to the car.

With Tina on her lap, Sarah had to lean sideways to get her phone out of her coat pocket. Ansel tried to give her room, but with me sitting on top of him, there wasn't much space to maneuver. The backseat was a rocky sea of arms and knees and shoulders.

Sarah's mom had left two text messages and two phone messages in a voice so shrill everyone in the car could hear it. She was upset. No one knew where we'd gone. Sarah thumbed her mother a reply and dropped the phone into her bag. "What did you tell her," I said.

"That I'd be home in an hour or so. The rest can wait. But you'd better turn your phone on. She says your father's been trying to reach you."

I waited until after we were on the New Jersey Turnpike to call him. He wanted to know where I'd gone, of course, although he suspected it had something to do with Brooklyn. When I told him that Ansel had driven us, he went from upset to ballistic. He calmed down a bit when I explained about Delores and the children, but he told me to tell Ansel to get off the turnpike immediately and park the car. He was coming to get us. His voice was so loud, even Clover turned toward me from the front seat.

"It's okay, Dad. Ansel's not driving."

"Then who the hell is driving? Not that old woman?"

"Mr. Mulvaney."

Everyone in the car seemed to hold their breath, waiting for my father's response. But he didn't say anything. I waited for him to protest or tell me Mr. Mulvaney couldn't come to our house. If he said anything like that, he was going to be in for a hard time.

"Is Mom still in New York?" I said.

"Yes," he said. "She's going to be staying there for a while. She wants you to call her."

"Yeah, sure," I said. One of these days.

"She talked to Eric. He's going to take care of the house."

Before we hung up, he told me to be careful another sixteen times and asked how old Delores's kids were.

When I closed the phone, no one asked me anything. Even Clover stayed quiet. We listened to Delores answer questions from John and Tina about the places we were passing. I couldn't help wondering what everyone was thinking, whether they'd been as frightened as I was through all this. My hands were still trembling and I felt lightheaded, almost weightless. Ansel kept rubbing my shoulder. Maybe he could feel the tension. I was glad to be heading home, to know that Delores and the children would be safe now.

Sarah's phone rang. It was her mother. "I'd better answer it," she said.

We could hear snippets of Mrs. Richardson's high-pitched voice as we listened to Sarah saying, "Yes, Mom; no, Mom" until finally she closed the phone and leaned toward the front seat. "You're in for a treat, Mr. Mulvaney. My mother wants to meet you."

"Do we need to stop at a mall? Get him outfitted?" said Ansel.

Sarah and I stopped laughing long enough to explain Mrs. Richardson's obsession with designer clothes. Mr. Mulvaney chuckled but had nothing to say about meeting her.

"What's going on?" I said to Sarah.

"I'm not sure. She said she'd see us at your house."

"I hope this doesn't turn into a pile-on," said Ansel. "I'd like to get the car back home without needing crowd control."

The house smelled of pizza, and the coffee table was piled high with storybooks, puzzles, and games that my father had run out and bought. Sarah and Delores seemed just as grateful as I was to be back safely, and at once the room filled with talk, one excited voice tripping over the next.

I described to my father how well Ansel drove, and Dad went into a mini-lecture about respect for the laws of physics and the skill of maneuvering around drivers who chose to defy the principle that two objects can't occupy the same space at one time. Ansel was more concerned about the laws of the Department of Motor Vehicles and what the State of New Jersey would think of his excursion if they knew.

The doorbell rang and Louisa soon appeared with Mrs. Richardson. My father took care of the introductions, keeping Mr. Mulvaney's identity deliberately vague. If Mrs. Richardson found something amiss, she was at least gracious enough not to ask questions. In fact, she seemed genuinely excited to meet him, almost deferential. "Mr. Mulvaney, I can't tell you how pleased I am that we're able to meet," she told him. "I have very exciting news."

Mr. Mulvaney looked a bit lost. "A pleasure to meet you," he assured her.

"As soon as I saw your drawings, I knew I wanted to represent you," she said. That wasn't exactly true, but I saw no need to correct the record. "I already have a meeting set up with a vendor I think will be very interested."

"Interested?" said Mr. Mulvaney.

"Yes, in displaying them. It's an Irish coffee and alehouse in Lambertville. Just opened. Of course, I know it's a modest start, but these venues can garner attention. I don't think a small gallery is out of the question for long."

"Oh, Mr. Mulvaney, that's wonderful," I said.

"You mean hanging them up for people to buy?" he said. "Is that what you're talking about?"

Mrs. Richardson seemed baffled that he didn't understand.

"Now, what else would they be hangin' 'em for?" said Clover. "Don't be a donkey," she whispered.

"Yes, Mr. Mulvaney. They would display them for an agreed period of time. Now, of course, they earn a percentage of the price if anything sells, but it's very small."

"Well, I don't know what to say."

"You can think about it," said Mrs. Richardson, probably because she thought Mr. Mulvaney was undecided. "If you decide you want to go ahead, I'll draw up a contract."

"That's a fine idea," said Clover. "You go right ahead and draw one."

"Yes," said Mr. Mulvaney. "I'm flattered is all."

"Well, we'll need to choose which drawings to use. That's one of the reasons I wanted to see you. Of course, the framed drawings you sent are truly excellent, but so are some of these." She held up the envelope my father and I had brought back from Brooklyn. Her excitement was contagious. Everyone followed her to the couch as she took the drawings out and displayed them one by one, offering her thoughts. She clearly had favorites. But I could see it was important to her that Mr. Mulvaney agreed with her choices.

Mr. Mulvaney didn't give her much to go on. He was a hard man to read, and I was sure he was a very different breed of cat from the people she was accustomed to working with. He seemed neutral, almost indifferent, about which ones she chose to display, at least until she took out the one of a woman with a baby. The woman was sitting on a bench with the child in her arms, a stroller pulled close. I recognized where she was. Penn Station. He had caught the woman as she was looking up, maybe at the board, expectant but sad.

"That's a nice one," said Ansel. "Did you do that from a photograph, too?" Nearly all his close-ups of people had been done from photos. But not that one.

"No," he said. "I did that from memory."

Everyone agreed it was among the best. I wasn't sure if anyone but me understood who the woman was. And I realized he had to have been there in Penn Station that day, watching my mother wait for him.

"I'd rather that not be sold," he said to Mrs. Richardson.

She immediately placed the drawing back into the envelope. "That's fine, Mr. Mulvaney. We have more than enough here."

"And there's more where that came from," said Clover. "Why, it'll be a pleasure to have some closet space again." I could see she was as happy for him as I was.

"Delightful," said Mrs. Richardson, and finished with a handshake, explaining to Mr. Mulvaney what would happen next. Mrs. Richardson had Sarah help her gather up the drawings and declined my father's invitation to stay for pizza. Sarah gave me a look over her shoulder as they left. I hoped our Brooklyn thrill ride wouldn't get her into too much trouble.

My father tried to herd the rest of us into the dining room, but Mr. Mulvaney hung back. "Won't you join us?" my father said.

"I have to catch a train. Perhaps a ride to the station?"

"There's time enough for that," Dad said with a glance toward me. "If you need to get back to Brooklyn, I'll drive you there later."

Mr. Mulvaney nodded, and we settled into the dining room. I tried to nibble on a slice, but I couldn't eat.

"Well then," said Clover to the children. "We've done enough today, haven't we?"

I looked at Mr. Mulvaney, who wasn't eating either. He had turned toward the window. I wondered if he was as confused as I was about what to think of all this. His gaze was fixed on the street. He seemed puzzled but expectant, as if surely the next car, the next passerby, would help everything make sense.

"Tell us a story, Clover," said John. He had grown restless, having eaten his fill. "A hero story."

"A hero story? We've no need for a story. Haven't we got a real hero right here with us?" said Clover. "Terence is our hero today. Terence and Maud's father, too, for taking us in." Her bony fingers reached over to squeeze my hand. Mr. Mulvaney turned from the window, the start of a smile on his face.

"I'm no hero," he said, glancing again at the cars heading home. Absently, he straightened Tina's hair as she stood beside his chair.

"You are, indeed," said Clover.

Delores took John onto her lap, pulled him close, nuzzled her face in his hair. She leaned back into the chair, able to relax finally in the safety they'd found.

Mr. Mulvaney looked at me with such tenderness. "Maud is your hero," he said, his voice no more than a whisper.

"I'm very proud of you, Maud," my father said, and I smiled at him. He put his hand on Mr. Mulvaney's shoulder, and something in the line of the old man's mouth softened. He looked rested, the way people look when they've returned from being away a long time and haven't yet gotten caught up in their old routines.

I saw Mr. Mulvaney a lot after that. In fact, with all my trips to Brooklyn, I got to be a really good driver—once I got my license. And his drawings were a big hit in Lambertville. Even Ansel's parents bought one. He gave me one to hang in my room. It was among a large stash he didn't show us at first, all done from photographs of me that he'd gotten from Uncle Peter. This one was done from a photo taken at the party after my kindergarten graduation. I'm eating cake and there's chocolate on my chin, a mortarboard askew, big smile.

Clover and Mr. Mulvaney never did get married, but by then I knew there were things people did that made no sense, things that kept them from having what they truly wanted. Like when Delores went to live with her husband yet again. It was such a crazy thing to do, but she didn't stay. She went back to school, and Clover watched the kids for her. She learned her lesson.

I wish I could say I learned mine. I never did tell Ansel the truth about Chicago, so I always felt like someone in disguise, like he never really knew me. We dated for almost a year, and maybe he would have found someone else anyway, but I'll always wonder if that's the way it had to be.

My mom never came back home. She stayed in New York. I saw her almost every week, when she wasn't traveling. Her car would be waiting for me in the same spot on the corner after school. I didn't want her to be apart from me and Dad, but we couldn't change her mind. She'd never talk about Mr. Mulvaney, but when I'd ask her if she'd come with me to see him, she'd say no in a way that made me wonder if what she really wanted was something else altogether.

about the author

Mary Ann McGuigan is the author of three previous novels for young adults, including *Where You Belong,* a finalist for the National Book Award, and its sequel, *Morning in a Different Place,* a Junior Library Guild selection. Her books have been ranked among the best books for teens by the New York Public Library, the Paterson Prize, and others, and she has served on the panel of judges for the National Book Award for Young People's Literature. She also writes short fiction for adults. She taught English after graduating from college and was a business and finance editor at Bloomberg L.P. for most of her career. A native of the Bronx, New York, she grew up there and in Jersey City, where she lives now. To find out more about her fiction, visit *www.maryannmcguigan.com.*